KATHRYN

MAIL-ORDER BRIDES OF SAPPHIRE SPRINGS

MARGERY SCOTT

Digital ISBN: 978-1-988191-19-5

Print ISBN: 978-1-988191-45-4

Sally

Anna

Beth

Willa

ROCKY RIDGE ROMANCE

It isn't only the Morgan men who fall in love in Rocky Ridge.

Landry's Back in Town

Substitute Bride

Wanted: The Perfect Husband

Hannah's Hero

High Stakes Bride

Jasper's Runaway Bride

Mail-Order Melanie

MAIL-ORDER BRIDES OF SAPPHIRE SPRINGS

Miranda

Audra

Kathryn

Elise

Laura

Cassie

CONTEMPORARY ROMANTIC SUSPENSE

BEHIND THE BADGE

A Time for Secrets

No One to Tell

The Stranger She Knows

A Question of Guilt

A Stranger in Paradise

CHAPTER 1

The rattle of wagon wheels on the rutted path leading to the house drew Pete Fallon's attention. He looked through the window of the shed he used as a workshop, smiling when he recognized his visitor—his best friend, John Weaver.

He didn't see John much these days. When he stopped to think about it, he didn't see any of his old friends as much as he used to. Now, he was the only unmarried man left in the group he'd grown up with in Sapphire Springs.

Surprised to see John at this time of day, he opened the shed door. A blast of cold air greeted him.

"What brings you out here?" Pete asked once John was inside.

"Miranda sent me to invite you to supper after church on Sunday," John told him.

"Why? What's the occasion?"

Pete looked away. "No occasion."

Pete had known John since they were barely out of diapers and by the way John was studying the grain on the surface of the bureau beside him, Pete knew there was something behind the invitation. "Who else is coming?"

John turned away and ran his hand over the smooth surface of the table. "Well…" he muttered, "Neall and Audra, Sam and Dorothy…"

Three couples. An even number. He'd be number seven. Miranda wouldn't invite him unless she'd also invited an unmarried—and eligible—woman to even out the numbers. "And?"

"Dorothy's sister, Agatha, is in town…" John mumbled.

Just as he'd thought. His friends were trying to marry him off. Again.

Not a chance! "Tell Miranda I died, or I've got the plague or…tell her whatever you want to, but I'm not spending one more minute with that woman than I have to. Have your forgotten what happened the last time you talked me into having supper with her? She'd already picked out our children's names before we even had dessert."

"She's a nice woman…and it's time you settle down, get yourself a wife, have a few kids—"

"Why?"

"Who's going to take over your farm when you're too old and feeble to do it yourself? And who are you going to teach to build furniture like you do? Besides, you might have enough women to warm your bed right now, but when you're wrinkled and bald and have one foot in the grave, that bed's going to be cold and empty."

"That might be so, but I don't need a woman nagging at me, or complaining that I don't bring in enough money to buy her all the frilly things she wants, or telling me what a sorry excuse I am for a man." He'd heard those words coming out of his mother's mouth every day for years until his father had had enough and had left a note on the kitchen table one afternoon when Pete was twelve years old. They'd never seen him again.

"You saying Miranda's a nag?"

Pete laughed. "Nah, you just got lucky."

"I did, but you were just unlucky with the ma you had. My ma wasn't anything like that. Don't tar all women with the same brush. Dorothy's sister——"

"Will not be seeing me at the same supper table that she's at. Thank Miranda for the invite, but I'll pass. Now, do you have time for a cup of coffee?"

"Thanks, but I don't. The girls want to play the new song Miranda taught them on the piano before they go to bed, so I'd best be getting back."

John moved to the door. He wrapped his fingers around the handle, then looked back over his shoulder. "Think about it, and if you change your mind…"

"I guarantee I won't."

John nodded and opened the door, lowered his head against the wind and hurried away, pulling the door closed behind him.

Pete moved to the window and watched him go until the wagon disappeared around a bend in the road. He shook his head at John and Miranda's invitation. Surely they knew he wouldn't be in any hurry to spend time with Agatha Trimble again.

He turned away from the window and crossed the large room to where he'd been carving egg-and-dart molding into the edge of a dressing table for a customer in Austin.

Where was the gouge he'd been using? He'd had it in his hand when he'd heard John's wagon. What had he done with it? He sighed. It had to be there somewhere.

It took almost five minutes of searching before he finally found it in an open drawer of a chest he'd been working on earlier that morning. He must have put it there just before he'd opened the door for John.

He went back to work, carefully using the gouge to finish the design on the dressing table.

As he worked, his thoughts wandered back to what John had said.

John was wrong. Pete didn't need a woman. He was happy with his life. When he wasn't working the small parcel of land he'd inherited when his mother passed away, he spent his days in the shed out behind his house. His reputation for building fine furniture was spreading to the point he had more work than he could handle. He had enough money to get by, and that was all he needed. He could do what he wanted, when he wanted, without having to account to anybody or be criticized for his faults. And he had female company when the mood struck him without having to make any promises.

Yeah, he'd worry about his old age when the time came.

The bell jingled again, the fifth time in less than a half hour. Kathryn Higgins leaned against the counter in the kitchen and let out a sigh. She loved her father. She really did. But sometimes the constant demands and complaints made her want to run screaming out of the house and as far away from Ohio as her legs could carry her.

She wouldn't do it, of course, but deep down, when she allowed the dreams to take root in her mind, she craved a life of her own, a home of her own, a family of her own …

She'd mentioned leaving once, and her father had become so distraught she'd thought he was going to have a stroke right in front of her eyes.

Slowly, she straightened and climbed the stairs. He was propped up in bed, pillows behind his head, his breakfast tray across his lap. "What is it, Papa?" she asked.

"When's Doc coming?"

"He said he'd stop by this morning sometime."

"I need to be washed and my hair combed before he gets here."

"I'll be back to do that as soon as I finish my breakfast. Are you finished with yours?"

He shook his head. "I couldn't eat it," he said. "The porridge was lumpy and my coffee is cold."

If you hadn't left it for a half hour, she wanted to point out. Instead, she clamped her lips shut and crossed to the bed. "Do you want more coffee?" she asked quietly as she picked up the tray and turned to leave.

"That would be nice," he replied. "I don't know what I'd do without you," she heard him say as she went back downstairs.

She'd just finished her own bowl of cold porridge when a knock came to the door. Dr. Lawson stood on the porch, his white hair disheveled, fatigue showing in his eyes. She was surprised to see him at this time of the morning, but she couldn't very well turn him away until she'd had time to make her father presentable. She'd hear about it later, though. "Come in, Doctor," she said, opening the door wide.

"I apologize for stopping in so early, but I've been up all night delivering Mrs. Gradwell's twins so I decided to check on your father before I head home."

"That's quite all right. You must be exhausted," Kathryn said sympathetically. She knew the doctor was at least ten years older than her father, yet he was never too tired to make a house call. "Can I get you a cup of coffee or something to eat?"

"No, but thanks for the offer." He took off his hat

and hung it on the hook behind the front door. "Is your father still in bed?"

She nodded.

He made a sound that almost sounded like disapproval and trudged over to the stairs. "I'll just go up now then," he said, gripping the banister and hauling himself up to her father's bedroom while Kathryn went back into the kitchen to clean up the breakfast dishes.

She was scrubbing the porridge pot when she heard the doctor's footsteps on the stairs a few minutes later. Drying her hands on a towel, she hurried through to meet him in the foyer. "How is he, Doctor?" she asked.

"He'd do a lot better if he'd get himself out of bed and start moving."

"Excuse me?"

He scrubbed a hand through his sparse white hair. "I've been treating your father for years, and I can't find a thing wrong with him that couldn't be cured with a little fresh air and exercise."

"That's not possible...his rheumatism...his muscles...he's so frail. I can see that when I wash him..."

"They've shrunk because he doesn't use them. Same with his joints. They need to be used to function properly." He took Kathryn's hand in one of his and patted it kindly with his other hand. "You're a good daughter, Kathryn, but you're not helping him when you run after him hand and foot. He needs to do for himself, and there's absolutely no reason he can't. He's not an old man. There's plenty of life left in him if he wants it."

"But—"

"When your mother died, it was as if he decided to give up on life. All he's done since the funeral is sit in that bed and let you do everything for him. And it's time to stop."

"He misses her…it was such a shock to his system…"

The doctor nodded. "I know that, and I'm not telling him not to grieve. But he's going to be joining her soon if he doesn't do something about it."

"Did you tell him this?"

He nodded. "He told me to get out and not come back."

Kathryn gasped. "He didn't!"

"He did, and I won't be back unless there's something really wrong. I have other patients who need me. Your father doesn't, at least not yet. He will if he doesn't change, though. He'll be sick…or worse. I likely shouldn't be telling you this, but you have to stop letting him use you as a maid. It's not your fault, but what you're doing is making him worse and it'll eventually kill him. Now I have to go and get some sleep before my clinic this afternoon." Again, he patted her hand. "You're a young woman who should already have a husband and family of your own. Don't let your father ruin your chances."

With that last piece of advice, he plucked his hat

off the hook and gave her a gentle smile before he walked out.

Kathryn closed the door and rested against it, the doctor's words spinning through her brain. Was she really making her father's health worse by taking care of him? How could she just desert him?

Her father's voice split the silence. "Kathryn! Come up here! And bring me another cup of coffee!"

Night had fallen by the time Pete blew out the lamp and left the shed. Clouds partly hid the moon, but there was enough light to see as he made his way across the yard to the house.

It was in darkness, and when he opened the door, for the first time, he noticed the emptiness in the house. No fire blazed in the fireplace. There was no aroma of supper cooking on the stove. No one to greet him and ask how his day had gone.

He was alone, and he always would be.

He'd never really thought about it before, but since John's visit, he hadn't been able to get it out of his mind.

He always had plenty of female companionship when he wanted it, and he'd always been quite content to look after himself. So why was it bothering him tonight?

He shivered as he piled old newspapers and kindling in the fireplace and added a log on top, then struck a match on the sole of his boot and held it against the newspapers, gazing absently as the flames took hold.

Then he went into the kitchen and found a loaf of bread and a block of cheese. That would have to do for supper since he didn't have the energy to cook. Not that he could cook much anyway. Eggs and stew. Those were the only things he knew how to make, and even those were barely edible.

After he finished eating, he went upstairs to his bedroom and stripped off his clothes before he slid between the sheets.

There was no warm woman beside him tonight, and if Pete was right, there would come a time when there would never be a woman in his bed again.

Maybe it was time to find a wife. He'd never really thought about being with one woman for more than a few weeks. Being faithful to one woman for the rest of his life.

Somehow, the idea of it wasn't as terrifying as he'd once thought it was. In fact, having a woman who was willing to spend her life with him wouldn't be such a bad thing. But where was he going to find one? There were very few unmarried ladies in Sapphire Springs, and he wasn't interested in those who were.

Both John and Neall had brought mail-order brides to Texas. John had first brought Miranda, and then Neall had asked for Miranda's help to find his bride, Audra.

Neall and John were happy with their new families. Was it possible Miranda could find him a bride, too?

He wouldn't love her. He wasn't capable of loving a woman. He knew that. He'd tried to fall in love and hadn't been able to, at least not enough to ever think about spending his life with that one woman.

Love was for fools. Love had made his father a victim. His father had loved his mother so much he'd put up with years of criticism and nagging trying to make the woman happy. And failing.

He rolled over, tugging the quilt tight around his neck. He still wasn't sure about being attached to one woman for the rest of his life, but it would be nice to have someone to welcome him home at night, to cook for him and clean up after him. And to take care of his needs in the bedroom when the mood hit him.

He'd make sure she understood that he would take care of her and protect her, but love wasn't something she could expect. As long as she agreed to that, they could have a good life together and maybe one day have children of their own.

Yeah, he thought moments before sleep finally claimed him, maybe I'll take a trip into town and talk to Miranda about finding me a bride, too.

CHAPTER 2

Snow swirled around Kathryn as she hurried the three blocks to her sister's house a few days later. Her nose was numb from the frigid weather but after the morning she'd had running after her father, she needed some fresh air.

She missed the days when she and Charlotte used to curl up in their bed and giggle and chatter until the wee hours of the morning. Charlotte had married a banker the year before and now had twin baby girls. She'd told Kathryn that even though she cared for Owen, she didn't love him the way she thought a woman should love her husband. She'd also told her that at twenty-two, it was likely the last chance she'd have to escape a life of drudgery looking after her father.

Since Charlotte's marriage, care of the three-story brick house and her father had fallen on Kathryn's shoulders. Her father wouldn't tolerate having a housekeeper, and between cooking and caring for him and taking care of all the household chores, she was busy every waking minute.

But Kathryn didn't blame her sister for taking the opportunity to have a life of her own. She only wished she had the courage to do the same thing—to leave, to live her own life, especially after what the doctor had told her.

Charlotte's face split into a wide smile when she opened the door to Kathryn's knock. She threw her arms around Kathryn and dragged her inside out of the cold. "It's so good to see you," she said. "But you're frozen. Why would you come outside on a day like this?"

Kathryn loved to visit Charlotte's house. It was small, but always gave her a warm, cozy feeling, something she missed at home since her mother died two years before. The aroma of cinnamon hung in the air.

"I just...I needed to get out of the house for a little while, and I miss you."

"I miss you, too," Charlotte said. "I just took an apple pie out of the oven. Take off your wet clothes and sit down by the fire and warm up. I'll make us some tea and we can catch up."

While Charlotte prepared the tea and sliced the pie, Kathryn settled into an armchair facing the fire and rubbed her hands together to get the circulation back.

"How's Papa?" Charlotte asked as she set two places at the small dining table.

"He's fine," Kathryn replied. "That's what I wanted to talk to you about."

The doctor's words had been preying on Kathryn's mind ever since the doctor left. She hadn't been strong-willed enough to refuse to care for her father, regardless of what the doctor had told her, and her father had been even more ill-tempered, taking out his anger with his doctor on her.

She was so tempted to tell her father she was leaving, but what if her father really was ill? What if the doctor was wrong and her father's ailments were because of illness and not lack of use? How could she live with herself if she deserted him and caused his death?

Charlotte's soft voice interrupted her thoughts. "Come and have some pie and tea and tell me what's wrong."

Kathryn got up and padded across the room to the table, slipping into the chair closest to the fire. Charlotte set a plate with a large slice of apple pie in front of her and poured tea into a china cup that had belonged to their mother. A bittersweet smile tweaked her lips as she grazed the floral pattern on the cup with her thumb.

"I thought it would be nice to use Mama's cups today," Charlotte said.

Kathryn added sugar and milk to her tea. "It is

nice. I only wish Mama was still here to enjoy tea with us."

Charlotte nodded slightly, then said, "This must be bad," a few seconds later. "You only put sugar and milk in your tea when you're upset."

Kathryn nodded. "I am, and I don't know what to do." For the next few minutes, Kathryn repeated everything the doctor had told her, and what her father's reaction had been when she'd tried to speak to him about the doctor's diagnosis the next day.

"The man's a quack," he'd said. "Doesn't know a boil from a nosebleed. I'm sick, and if you were any kind of daughter, you'd take my word over a stranger's."

Charlotte sipped at her tea, faint lines appearing between her brows. She was thinking, Kathryn knew.

"I can't desert him, but if Dr. Lawson is right…" Kathryn went on. A lump formed in her throat, and tears spilled over and trickled down her cheeks. "If he's right…and I think he is…I'm killing him…"

"I'm so sorry," Charlotte said, a pained expression filling her face. "I should never have left you with the burden of looking after him."

"Don't be silly." Kathryn adjusted the spoon she'd been using to stir her tea. "I told you on your wedding day, and I've told you the same thing every time you've brought it up since. You were lucky enough to find a good man who wanted to spend his life with you. I don't blame you one bit for wanting to marry him. When will you believe me?"

"I'm not sure I would have been so understanding if it had been you who'd found a husband first."

"Of course you would. Now, tell me what to do. I'm afraid no matter what I do, it's the wrong thing."

"I think you already know what you have to do. You have to leave."

Kathryn's heartbeat tripled. "Oh…no…I can't do that…"

Charlotte leaned across the table and rested her hand on top of Kathryn's. "You can. You have to."

"What if the doctor is wrong? What if—?"

"If he's wrong, I'll be here. I won't live with him, but Owen can afford to hire someone to care for him. If he's right, however, he'll eventually get back to being the man he used to be."

"But what will I do?" Kathryn's voice rose and her heart raced at the likelihood she'd be homeless. "I have no skills…nowhere to go…"

Charlotte got up and disappeared into the parlor, returning a minute later with a newspaper in her hand. She opened it, flipped the pages until she found what she was looking for. "Here," she said, folding the newspaper and sliding it in front of Kathryn. She pointed to a small advertisement near the bottom of the page.

Kathryn's eyes widened when she read the small print.

"Carpenter, 28, healthy and decent, far from rich but can support a wife and children, looking for a woman 20-25 years old who is healthy and capable of looking after a home and family (eventually) to be my bride. If you are that woman, please reply to Mrs. Miranda Weaver, Sapphire Springs, Texas."

Kathryn shoved the newspaper away as if it was on fire. "You can't be serious."

"I am," she said, pushing the newspaper back to Kathryn. "It's the perfect solution. You need to get away from Papa but you have no way to support yourself."

"But I can't marry a stranger… What if he's like Papa? Or worse? What if he drinks, or beats me, or—?"

"If that happens, you leave and come home and we'll figure something else out."

"I don't know…"

"I'll miss you so much, but as long as you're here and not married, Papa will expect you to look after him for the rest of his days. You know that. You'll never have a life of your own."

Kathryn let out a sigh of resignation. Charlotte was right. If only Texas wasn't so far away. "I know that, but I can't leave everything and everyone I love to go all that way. I just can't."

Kathryn left soon after, her thoughts jumbled, flitting from the problem of her father to Charlotte's suggestion that she travel to Texas to marry a man she'd never met. Charlotte had tucked the newspaper under Kathryn's arm as she'd walked out the door.

"Where have you been?" Her father's voice carried down the stairs the moment she opened the front door. "You know I need you to be close by in case I get one of my spells."

"Yes, Papa," she called out as she unwound the scarf from around her neck and hung it with her coat on the hook behind the door.

"Come up here and get my book for me."

"I'll be right there."

Slowly, she climbed the stairs. This was to be her life, being at the beck and call of a man who might or might not be the invalid he thought he was.

"It's on the bureau," he said when she went into the room. "I tried to get it myself and fell out of bed. I called for you but you'd gone out."

"I told you I was going to visit Charlotte."

"You said you wouldn't be long."

Kathryn looked at the clock. She'd been gone only a little more than an hour. Surely he could have waited for his book until she got back.

"Here you are," she said, picking the book up from the bureau and handing it to him. "I'll go and start supper."

"On second thought, I don't want the book now. I'm too tired to read."

Kathryn went back downstairs and headed to the kitchen. As she browned meat for the stew she was planning for supper, her eyes strayed to the newspaper she'd left on the kitchen table.

Could she really do this? Could she really marry a man she didn't know? She read the advertisement again.

"Kathryn? Bring me a glass of water!" Her father's voice reached her again.

This would be her life unless she did something about it. As much as she loved her father and would miss him, if the doctor was right, surely one day he'd see she was leaving him out of love.

She got her father the water he wanted, then quickly chopped the other ingredients for the stew. Once it was simmering gently on the stove, she took a piece of paper from the desk in her father's study— the study he hadn't entered since the day her mother died. For a few moments, she stared at the blank page, then dipped her pen into the ink and began to write.

Pete drew the wagon to a halt in front of The Blue Sapphire Diner and hopped down. He'd finished the cabinet John had ordered as a surprise for Miranda, and it was wrapped tightly in the wagon bed. He wouldn't unload it until he was sure Miranda wasn't in the diner.

The bell jingled when he went inside, stopping to sniff at the aroma of roasting chicken coming from the kitchen.

The diner was empty other than two cowboys at one of the corner tables. Pete had planned it that way, so that he'd get there during the quietest part of the day.

John's head poked through the opening between

the kitchen and the eating area. A frown creased his forehead and Pete caught the slight shake of his head, which meant this was not the time to unload the cabinet. "How's it going, Pete?" John asked. "You want some supper?"

Okay, Pete thought, he could take a hint. "If you're sure the chicken I'm smelling won't kill me," he replied with a laugh.

"No worse than yours."

"Ha!"

"I'll dish you out a plate."

The door between the kitchen and the eating area opened and Miranda walked out. "Hello, Pete. It's so good to see you. I was going to send John out to your place later with some letters for you."

"Letters, as in more than one?"

Miranda chuckled. "Several."

"Would it be all right if I look at them now while I eat?"

"Of course," she said with a smile. "I'll fetch them right now."

Pete had seen the ad before Miranda had sent it off. He'd figured one, maybe two, women might be desperate enough to write back. He'd made a point of making himself look as poor as possible so he wouldn't have to risk any woman with money responding. He didn't want to end up like his father, with a woman who'd expect luxury and spend her days complaining about it if he didn't provide it.

While Miranda was getting the mail, Pete took off

his jacket and draped it over the back of a chair at a table near the window.

He'd barely sat down when Miranda appeared with a cup of coffee and put it in front of him. She dug into the pocket of her apron and took out several envelopes. "Here you are," she said, setting them on the table beside the coffee. "Eight of them, and there may be more on the next stage."

"Thanks, Miranda," he called out as she walked away. He picked up the envelopes, glancing through them. He wasn't sure why he felt it was important to look at the envelopes. Was it because he was trying to postpone opening them? Which brought up another question—why didn't he want to open the letters?

He had no answer so while he waited for his meal to arrive, he began. The first letter he read was from a woman in Ohio who was anxious to come to Texas to begin a new life. She was a good cook and house-keeper, and was anxious to have a home of her own. She said she was eager to be his helpmate and to care for him with the hope that one day, love might blossom between them. If not, she would always treat him with respect and kindness.

As he read the other letters in the pile, he was drawn back to that first letter. It bothered him that she was hoping for love in the future, the one thing he couldn't provide. Still, he couldn't say why, but some-thing about the way she wrote gave him a sense of calmness, of peace and something he couldn't define.

He'd told Miranda he wasn't ready to commit

himself to marriage, but as his imagination conjured up a vision of the woman who'd written the letter, he found himself wanting to get to know her better.

His meal arrived, and he ate quickly, anxious to get back to his house where he could really think about the possibility of marriage.

He was about to leave when John approached, glancing furtively around to make sure Miranda wasn't within earshot.

"Miranda is going to visit my aunt tomorrow for the day. I can bring the wagon and pick up the cabinet."

"It's already in mine, so I'll just bring it back then rather than unloading it and loading it into yours in the morning."

"Thanks. Sorry about today."

"No problem," Pete said, getting up and shoving his sleeves into his jacket. "I'm glad I came and got the letters from Miranda."

"Find a woman you want to bring out here?"

"Not me," Pete told him. He wasn't about to tell anyone the direction his thoughts were going. Not yet. Not until he'd thought it through. Just because John and Neall had found brides they'd fallen in love with, they were anxious to get him married off, too. That was not going to happen until he was good and ready.

A few snow flurries drifted down when he left the diner and drove home. He unharnessed his horses, rubbed them down and fed them, then went into the house and built a fire. He dropped into the armchair beside the fireplace and tugged off his boots, then leaned back and closed his eyes. The evening stretched out in front of him, long and silent.

No conversation, no laughter, just his own thoughts.

He understood why his friends got married. The difference was, he didn't really need someone to cook and clean for him. He could do that for himself…well, he could clean for himself. Cooking was something else, but he could always eat at the diner. What he did miss was companionship to fill the silence.

He'd never really noticed the quiet until lately, but now that he had…

He could go to the saloon. He'd find noise there. And plenty of female company…if he was willing to pay for it. He wasn't.

He got up and dug Kathryn's letter out of his pocket. He stood, his back to the fireplace, and read the letter again.

A short time later, he sat down at the table and composed a reply to Miss Kathryn Higgins. If she accepted his proposal, she'd soon be Mrs. Pete Fallon.

CHAPTER 3

"Now I wish I'd never convinced you to write to this…Pete Fallon. The train will be here any minute and you'll leave and Heaven only knows how long it'll be before we'll see each other again."

Kathryn smiled gently at Charlotte, tucked her arm in Charlotte's elbow and quickly drew her out of the way before a beefy man hurrying along the platform knocked her off balance. "I hope I'm doing what's best for Papa," she said once they were safely out of the way. "I'm only sorry you may get the brunt of his anger once he reads the letter."

Charlotte's eyes widened. "Letter? What letter? You didn't tell him you were leaving?"

Kathryn's head drooped. "I couldn't. You know Papa. He'd make me feel so guilty I'd end up staying. I am going to miss him, though, and I hope that Dr.

Lawson is right and he'll go back to being the man—and the father—he was when Mama was alive. I'm sorry. I should have told him—"

"He'll be furious, but I don't live there. At least I can leave."

"Do that," Kathryn said. "Please don't let him rant at you because of what I've done."

"I won't." Charlotte wrapped her woolen scarf tighter around her neck. "At least it's warmer in Texas than it is here from what I hear."

It was late April, but it had been a brutal winter, and still hadn't warmed to the temperature it usually was at this time of year.

"I hope so," Kathryn agreed with a grin. "You know I'm always cold so Texas should be perfect for me."

A shrill whistle sounded and both women turned to watch the train chugging into the station. The brakes squealed and it came to a stop a few seconds later. The doors opened and passengers piled out, making the platform even more crowded. Kathryn and Charlotte were jostled and pushed until finally, the passengers who'd arrived on the train had left and many of those who were starting their journeys were already on board.

A deep, booming voice filled the air. "All aboard!"

A lump formed in Kathryn's throat and her eyes stung with tears. "I'd better go or the train will leave without me."

Charlotte nodded, her own tears trickling down her cheeks. "Remember, you don't have to put up with a man who mistreats you. If you want to come back and you don't have enough money, send me a telegram and I'll wire it to you."

"I will." Kathryn wrapped her sister in a long hug until the train whistle warned her she'd better hurry. "I love you," she murmured, then spun around and walked away before her sister could see her tears.

"I love you, too," Charlotte called out as Kathryn boarded the train that would carry her away from the only life she'd ever known.

Pete tugged at his shirt collar. It felt like a noose, and as the train approached the station, it felt as if it was getting tighter and tighter until he was sure that by the time the train arrived, it would be strangling him.

What had he done? He must have breathed in too much varnish to make him do something as asinine as proposing marriage to a woman he didn't even know.

But he'd done it, and he couldn't very well back out now. The woman had come all the way from Dayton to marry him. Which made him wonder what was wrong with her that she couldn't find a husband in Ohio.

He'd had plenty of experience with women, and he'd left a few broken hearts behind him through the years. So why did he feel like a schoolboy at his first dance? He laughed to himself. He hadn't even been this nervous at his first dance. He'd looked forward to holding a girl in his arms, and maybe stealing a kiss before the night was through.

But this was no dance. This was a commitment for life. And he'd made a promise to a woman he'd never met that he'd look after her and be faithful to her until the day he died.

Sweat pooled under his arms and trickled between his shoulder blades. Whether it was from the Sunday suit he was wearing or nerves, he didn't know.

Or more than likely he was sweating because he'd been sure he was late meeting the train. He hadn't been able to find his cufflinks. He'd worn them the Sunday before to church, but they'd disappeared. It had taken him almost an hour to find them in the kitchen behind the coffeepot.

The train had likely come and gone and his bride would be disappointed he wasn't there, wondering if he was going to show up at all. Or she'd be furious that he'd kept her waiting. Either way, it wasn't a good way to start.

He was still a half mile to town when he heard the train whistle in the distance. He plucked his pocket watch out and glanced at the time. The train was late. Thanking the heavens, he urged the horses to move faster, and by the time he drew the wagon to a stop at the small weathered building that functioned as the depot, he was sweating and the train was just pulling in.

With one last squeal and a burst of steam, the train hauling three passenger cars and two freight cars stopped. One of the passenger cars had curtains at the windows, and as the door opened, a man carrying a wooden step hurried out of the depot and set it down. Another man laid planks of wood stretching from the platform to the openings in the other cars. Pete had heard that trains these days had first-class cars for those passengers who were willing to pay more for comfort while they traveled.

Pete stood back, watching. Several passengers carefully made their way down the wood planks to the platform, none of them women. Three men and an elderly couple got off the car with the curtains at the windows and walked away. It was obvious by the way they were dressed that they had money. He didn't see anyone else, and for a few moments, wondered if maybe Kathryn had changed her mind about coming after all.

He couldn't decide if he was disappointed or relieved. He didn't have time to figure it out because suddenly, a woman appeared at the doorway where the conductor was waiting at the steps. Was that Kathryn?

The conductor reached out to take the woman's hand to escort her down the steps.

"I hope you had a pleasant trip, Miss Higgins," he heard the conductor say.

"I did, thank you," she replied. She smiled, and even though the smile wasn't directed at Pete, it did something to his heartbeat.

So this was Kathryn! And she'd gotten out of the first-class train car. That meant... Why hadn't she mentioned she had money?

She was much prettier than he expected, so it wasn't her looks that had stopped her finding a husband back in Ohio. The dark blue traveling suit she was wearing looked like it was made with fine silk and was trimmed with white lace that didn't have a smudge or mark on it. A matching hat sat perched on top of her dark brown curls. Why, her outfit likely cost more than he made in a month.

She was pale, but that wasn't unusual in northern folks. From what he'd heard, women up north carried parasols whenever they were outside. He hoped she didn't expect to do the same in Texas. It would be hard, if not impossible, for her to hang out laundry or do any of the other outside chores with a parasol in her hand.

Her eyes sparkled and he noticed a small dimple in her cheek when she smiled at the conductor.

He swore. Just the kind of woman he didn't need —a prissy, high-falutin' woman like his mother who'd never be satisfied with what he could provide.

Still, the smile she'd given the conductor had seemed genuine enough. And she was pretty. He'd give her that. His pa had always told him never to judge folks by how they looked, and he'd done his best to always look behind what showed. What would his pa think about him now, already deciding the woman was like his ma when he didn't even know her yet?

He needed to give her a chance. She'd show her true colors soon enough.

The conductor picked up the step and took it back into the depot while the other men removed the planks from the other passenger cars and piled them beside the building.

She stood quietly, her gaze uncertain as it scanned the few people still on the platform. Finally, her hazel eyes met Pete's and a flush stole over her creamy cheeks.

What was he supposed to say to her? For the first time in his life, he was tongue-tied around a woman. He couldn't leave her standing there, though. Sucking in a calming breath, he closed the gap between them. "Miss Higgins…Kathryn?"

She nodded, her smile widening. "Mr. Fallon?"

"I am," he said. "Welcome to Texas."

This was the man she'd agreed to marry? Kathryn's heartbeat skittered in her chest. He was … big, much bigger than she expected. Somehow, she'd assumed since he made furniture that he'd spend his days indoors. He'd be pale, like her father. Like her brother-in-law, Owen. His skin wouldn't be darkened by the sun, and his hair wouldn't have gold streaks mixed into the dark brown strands she'd noticed when he took off his hat.

Unlike Owen and her father, he was handsome. Far too handsome to not have women lined up to marry him. His dark eyes twinkled, and the tiny creases at the corners gave her the impression he smiled a lot. So why had he found it necessary to send away for a bride? Did he drink too much? Carouse? Was he a spendthrift? Did he have some flaw that all the women in Sapphire Springs were aware of and that was why he wasn't already married?

The letter she'd received from him along with a train ticket and money for travel implied he was prosperous enough to support a family, that he was a hard-working, responsible, church-going man.

His smile seemed to send heat scurrying through her veins, and his deep voice held a faint twang that she found easy to listen to. It was impossible to know what kind of man he was since he'd only said a few words to her, but he seemed nice enough so far. But his size … it frightened her. What if he had a violent temper? She'd known a woman who'd been victim to a man much smaller than Pete… If Pete was anything like the woman's husband, he could not only hurt her. He could kill her.

Don't think about that now. Concentrate on something else, something more pleasant.

His face glistened with perspiration. Not surprising, she thought, since she was overly warm, too. It was like a summer day here, and her traveling outfit was far too thick for these temperatures.

He cupped her elbow and led her along the platform toward the back of the train. "How was your journey?"

"Long, and tiring," she said. "And wonderful, although I admit I'm glad the noise and the constant rocking are done."

He chuckled. "I bet you are. It'll likely take a little while to get used to being still again, but you've still got some rocking to do in the wagon before we get to Sapphire Springs."

"That's quite all right." She gazed around. "At least I'll be able to breathe in fresh air, warm though it is."

"You are a bit flushed," he noted, his gaze sliding over her and making her blush. "I hope you have some thinner clothes with you."

"I did bring summer dresses. I just wasn't prepared for it to be so warm here so early in the year. This weather is like a July day in Ohio."

"I have water in a canteen in the wagon, but if you're hungry, we could stop and have something to eat before we set off?"

Kathryn shook her head. "I'm not, so unless you are, I'd rather leave now. I'm anxious to reach Sapphire Springs."

"Then let's get your baggage and we'll head out. We still have a two-hour ride ahead of us."

By the time they reached Sapphire Springs, the sun had dipped, hovering on the horizon, sending rays of gold and pink across the sky.

Pete drew the wagon to a stop in front of a small house beside a whitewashed church. "We're here," he said. "If you really want a church wedding with all the trimmings, I can get you a room at the hotel until we arrange it—"

This was it! Her heart thumped against her ribs and a thousand butterflies flitted around in her stomach. "No," she interrupted. "I appreciate the offer, but it's not necessary."

"If you're sure…"

No, she wasn't sure at all. In fact, she'd never been more unsure of anything in her life. This could be a huge mistake. But she'd traveled a long way to marry this man, and so far, she hadn't found any reason to go back on her promise.

He'd been a pleasant companion on the ride to town, telling her about himself and entertaining her with stories of the people who lived in Sapphire Springs. He hadn't been self-absorbed, though, like other men she'd known. He was a good listener and seemed to be genuinely interested in her life as well.

And he was so nice to just look at. He smiled often and his laugh warmed her insides.

"I'm sure."

"Then let's go get this done," he said with a grin

as he jumped out of the wagon and tied the horses to the hitching post.

Kathryn scooped up her skirt, wondering how exactly she was supposed to climb down out of the wagon. She'd never ridden in a wagon before, only in a carriage with someone to help her when she arrived at her destination.

She'd gingerly rested one foot on the hub of the wagon wheel to climb down when she felt two hands suddenly grip her waist. A fraction of a second later, she was lifted off her feet. She couldn't stop a tiny squeak escaping her mouth.

Pete gently lowered her to the ground. Their eyes met and her heart skipped a beat.

He held her for what felt like a long time before he released her, took her hand and began walking toward the house. "This is the preacher's house," he said. "He'll marry us."

Kathryn's legs were trembling so hard she was afraid she was going to crumple. Forcing one foot in front of the other, she let Pete lead her up the steps to a wide porch. The door opened before he had the chance to knock.

A man who reminded her of an elf she'd seen in a picture book when she was a little girl stood in the doorway. A wide smile transformed his face into a mass of creases. "There you are," he said. "I expected you hours ago."

"Sorry, Reverend. The train was late getting in," Pete said.

"And this must be your beautiful bride." The minister took Kathryn's hand. "Kathryn, isn't it?"

Kathryn nodded, her throat so dry she was afraid to try to speak.

"I'm Micah Ford," he said, "and the lovely lady behind me with the silverware in her hand is my wife, Tillie. It's a pleasure to meet you."

"Thank you," Kathryn croaked, heat rising in her cheeks as she cleared her throat. "It's nice to meet you, too."

"Well, don't leave them standing there, Micah," Tillie said with a grin, pushing past Micah to open the door wide. "Come on inside. You must both be exhausted after the trip back from Austin."

The aroma of roasted beef and apples met Kathryn's nose. Her stomach rumbled. Mortified, she slid a quick glance at the others to see if they'd heard it. If they had, they were polite enough to pretend they hadn't.

"We were just sitting down to supper," the reverend said. "Are you folks in a hurry to get married, or can you wait a few minutes?"

"We're in no rush."

Pete had answered so quickly, Kathryn had a sudden thought that maybe he didn't want to get married at all.

"I'll put out an extra two plates and you can join us before we get down to business. You must be starving by now."

Kathryn's stomach was in such knots she knew

that even though she was hungry, she likely wouldn't be able to swallow a bite. "Oh…no…we couldn't impose…"

The reverend waved away her objection. "Nonsense. We have more than enough." He smiled and leaned closer, pretending to whisper although Kathryn was sure his wife could hear every word. "In truth, I don't like leftovers so I'll be happy to make sure there aren't any."

"We appreciate the hospitality," Pete told him, taking off his hat and putting it on a table just inside the door.

The reverend clapped his hands together. "Good. Good. Now come on through and sit yourselves down."

For the next half hour, Kathryn sat quietly while Pete and the Fords chatted about the goings-on in town. The roast beef Tillie—the reverend's wife had insisted Kathryn call her by her first name—served were delicious, but Kathryn could only manage a few bites. When Tillie offered her a bowl of apple crisp a short time later, she was tempted. It was one of her favorite desserts, but she refused, worried she'd embarrass herself if she put anything more in her stomach.

Finally, the reverend got up and put his napkin on the table. "Well, Pete, are you ready? Your bride is either anxious to start married life or terrified, I'm not sure which."

Terrified didn't even begin to describe the emotions surging through her veins. Fear and worry but at the same time, excitement and anticipation.

"Come on through to the other room. You don't want to have a wedding in the midst of a pile of dirty dishes."

He led them through to a sitting room, small but the kind of room Kathryn could imagine curling up in with a book in front of the fireplace on a cold winter night. A thick carpet covered the floor and photographs and knick-knacks decorated the surfaces of the gleaming wood furniture. The aroma of the meal they'd just had lingered in the air.

Reverend Ford picked up a bible from a small table beside an overstuffed armchair. "Stand over here," he said, gesturing to a spot in front of the fireplace.

Pete rested his hand on the small of Kathryn's back and ushered her into place. His touch was gentle, but she felt a spark of…something she'd never felt before. Something quite exciting.

"Now join hands."

Pete buried her hands in his, his heat stealing up her arms and warming her through and through. The sensation was so heady she barely heard the reverend's words until Pete squeezed her hands and smiled down at her. "You having second thoughts?"

"What…oh…I'm sorry…no…"

The reverend gave her a kind smile. "It's a bit overwhelming, so just repeat after me. I, Kathryn …"

Kathryn recited the words that would commit her to Pete until one of them died, surprised that once she got started, her voice was clear and strong. She even managed a shy smile at Pete when she promised to be faithful to him for the rest of her life.

A short time later, the reverend announced that they were husband and wife. "If you've a mind to kiss your bride now, you can go right ahead."

Kathryn was glad the preacher was giving Pete a choice. The question was, did he want to? If he did decide to kiss her, it meant he was anxious to make this marriage work. If he didn't…

Pete gazed down at her for a few seconds that seemed to last an eternity before he lowered his lips to hers.

Her heart beat with the speed of a hummingbird's wings as his lips gently brushed against hers. This was the first time a man had kissed her, and a spark of heat surged through her. It was both exciting and terrifying at the same time. She'd never experienced such a sensation. Eyes wide, she gazed up at Pete, unable to speak.

When his lips left hers, her fingers reached up and touched her lips, wondering if they really were on fire. They definitely felt like they were.

She'd often wondered how a man's kisses could make a woman all light-headed and trembly the way she'd heard they did. Now she knew.

Pete's dark eyes were unreadable, but they held her gaze until the reverend cleared his throat. "If you two can tear your eyes off each other long enough to sign your marriage license, you can get started on the honeymoon sooner."

Pete broke their connection first, his eyes twinkling as he turned to the reverend and laughed. Then he looked back at Kathryn. "Let's get this signed so we can go home."

CHAPTER 4

$\mathcal{I}$diot! Why had he said that? By the terrified expression on Kathryn's face, he might as well have told her he was going to lynch her from the nearest tree.

Sure, he wouldn't mind if she was willing to make their marriage real as soon as they got back to his house, but he knew just from talking to Kathryn for the few hours on the way to town that even if she was willing enough, she wasn't ready for that side of marriage.

She was scared of him. That much was obvious. She'd been nervous when they'd first met at the train station, but she'd seemed to relax a little on the trip to town. But once they reached the Fords' house, she'd tensed up. She'd barely touched her supper, even though he'd heard her stomach rumble earlier so he knew she must have been hungry.

He understood why she was scared. She likely

hadn't had any experience with men, and she didn't know what to expect from their wedding night.

He'd had experience with women, but he didn't know how to handle a woman who was terrified of his lovemaking. He'd never met a woman who was scared of him before. In fact, he'd always had a knack for making people—especially women—relax and enjoy his company. And he'd sure never had a problem getting a woman into his bed. Until now.

When he told the Fords that it was time they left, she quietly let him lead her outside. She walked so slow he might as well have been leading her to the gallows.

By the time he loosened the horse's reins from the hitching post in front of the Fords' house, Kathryn had already climbed into the wagon and was staring straight ahead, her back stiff as a poker, her hands clasped so tight in her lap that her knuckles were white.

Having a wife who was terrified of him was no way to begin married life. Had Miranda and John started out like this? Or Neall and Audra?

"My farm is just at the other side of town," he said once he'd climbed onto the seat beside her and flicked the reins. "It's not very big, but—"

She twisted, a frown marring her creamy forehead. He caught a spark of anger in her voice. "Farm? What farm? You said you're a carpenter."

"I am a carpenter."

"Then what are you doing with a farm?"

He let out a short laugh. "Sorry, I call it that, but it's not really a farm," he corrected. "The house sits on a small parcel of land just outside town. I have vegetables and berries, a few fruit trees, some chickens and a milk cow. It's not big enough to support us, but for me, living alone, it was more than enough. Whatever vegetables, milk and eggs I didn't use myself, I gave to John and Miranda at the diner in exchange for meals or I sold them to the mercantile."

"Oh…"

"Did you think I was lying about being a carpenter?" he asked, his brows arching.

"Not at all," she replied.

He studied her face, and could see that was exactly what she'd thought. He reached out and took her hand. "I don't lie, Kathryn. I won't ever lie to you, no matter what. I am a carpenter. I earn enough to support us doing that. The farm is for us. It'll provide enough food that we won't have to buy much except flour and sugar and whatever else you need to cook with."

Worry filled her eyes.

"I grew up in the middle of a city," she said. I've never even seen a farm. I don't know how to grow anything, or look after animals. I did have a cat once for a little while, but I wasn't responsible for taking care of it."

"It's all right," he assured her. "I didn't expect you to know about farming. That's why I didn't mention it in the advertisement."

"What if I kill your vegetables?" Then she sucked in an audible gasp of horror. "Or even worse, your animals?"

She looked so beautiful, her eyes wide as her bottom teeth nibbled at her lip that he couldn't help but smile. That was the worst thing he could have done.

"It's not funny," she spat out. "I came out here assuming you'd spend your days in your workshop building whatever it is you build. I thought I'd only be responsible for cooking and cleaning. You didn't tell me I'd have to look after gardens and chickens… and…and…"

"I didn't tell you about the farm because I didn't want you to react the way you are right now and decide you didn't want to come out west."

"It might not have mattered," she countered.

His brows lifted. "Really? You expect me to believe that?"

"Well…"

"So no, I didn't tell you," he said. "I should have. I know that now, but it's not important. I don't expect you to look after it… unless you want to, that is."

Letting her know he wasn't going to work her to death seemed to be enough to ease the worry lines on her face.

"Oh…"

Soon, Pete turned off the trail. Night had already fallen, but the moonlight peeking from behind wispy clouds provided enough light for Kathryn to see a house and a few outbuildings in the distance. A few minutes later, he stopped the wagon in front of a two-story house with large windows. A porch ran all the way around the house, at least the part she could see. She assumed it covered the back of the house, too. A few flowers dotted the grass near the porch stairs.

In the shadowy light, she saw a large building and a barn near the house. Kathryn guessed the building was Pete's workshop.

It was hard to make out the details in the dark, but something about the house appealed to her, and she sensed she was going to like living here. The open space around her, the freshness of the air, the freedom…yes, she was going to be happy here.

Pete lifted her out of the wagon, and again, he left his hands on her waist a few seconds longer than he needed to.

Kathryn stood beside the wagon and gazed up at the dormers she'd noticed on the second floor. She'd always loved dormer windows. Her grandmother's house had had dormer windows with padded seats and cushions. When she'd stayed there as a young girl, she'd curled up there to read stories of faraway places and exciting adventures.

She smiled to herself. This was a real-life adventure. Would it end in a happily-ever-after? Only time would tell. "Your house is lovely, Pete," she said.

"I'm glad you like it. I hope you like the inside as well."

Taking her hand, he led her up the porch steps.

She was getting used to him holding her hand, and she had to admit it felt nice. She'd never thought a man's touch would be something she'd enjoy. Then again, the only time she'd felt a man's touch before Pete held her hand was when her father punished her.

"Miranda said I'm supposed to carry you over the threshold," Pete said as he opened the door. "If you'd rather I didn't, though…"

Her cheeks warmed at the thought of Pete's arms around her again. They were married now, and he had every right to do more to her than just hold her in his arms. And, she admitted to herself, she'd liked being in his arms when he'd lifted her out of the wagon. "I've heard it's for good luck, so I don't mind."

"Then we better do it," he said. "I wouldn't want to be responsible for any bad luck that comes our way."

Gently, he scooped her up in his arms and drew her close to his body.

Her heart raced and her breath caught in her throat. Wrapping her arms around his neck, she nuzzled her head into his neck, feeling his pulse against her cheek. His coffee-laced breath whispered across her face.

As he carried her through the door, his grip tightened, and even when he kicked the door shut behind him, he didn't put her down immediately. Instead, he bent his head toward hers. Was he going to kiss her again?

Heavens, she wanted him to!

As if he'd come to his senses, he lowered her gently to the floor. She stood facing him, watching the play of emotions cross his handsome face.

He cleared his throat. "Uh…here, I'll show you around."

She nodded, unsure what to say.

For the next few minutes, he took her through the house, holding her hand the entire time. The house was bigger than it appeared from the outside, and the main floor consisted of one large room holding a sofa and three armchairs at one end, and a dining table and six chairs at the other. A stone fireplace took up part of one wall. The furniture was heavy and well-made, although most of it was littered with newspapers and tools he'd obviously forgotten to leave in his workshop.

Was he looking for a housekeeper and not a wife? Her heart sank. Had she left the safety and security of her home and family only to land in a situation that was worse than the one she'd left?

"I've been really busy lately," he said. "I'm not usually this messy."

She hoped he was telling the truth.

She wandered through the room, pausing in front of a bookcase holding copies of many of the classics she'd read growing up. She was pleased to see he enjoyed reading, too.

She ran her hand across the top. The wood was smooth beneath her touch, and the carved designs along the front were intricate and expertly done. "Did you make this?" she asked.

He nodded. "I like to make things that are beautiful as well as useful."

"You're very talented."

Was that a flush she saw rising in his face? Was he not used to being complimented on his work?

"Just takes practice," he muttered.

She smiled. "I'm sure it does, but this work is more than just practice. Some people never find out what their talent is, but I truly believe everyone is born with at least one."

"Have you found yours?"

She gave him a wry smile. "Not yet. I'm still looking."

"Maybe you'll find it here."

"I'm sure I will."

Awkward silence filled the room. Kathryn turned away and strolled through the room, touching, admiring the large, yet cozy, space.

"You look tired," he said finally. "You've had a long journey."

Was this a hint that he was ready to claim his marital rights? Did she dare admit to being exhausted? She was far too nervous to sleep, so the longer she could postpone going to bed, the better. Still, she had to sleep sometime, so maybe it would be better to just get it over with.

As if he'd read her mind, he moved toward the door. "I'll get your things and take them upstairs."

She turned to face him. "Thank you. If you don't mind, I'll check to see what supplies you have on hand in the kitchen to make for breakfast in the morning."

While Pete went outside, Kathryn strolled into the kitchen. Like the rest of the house, it was messy, dishes taking up most of the worktable and part of a long counter stretching the length of the room.

Unless he had more dishes hidden away somewhere, she'd have to wash them in the morning before she could even think about making breakfast.

Ignoring the mess, she looked through the pantry cabinet in the kitchen. It was huge, and filled with everything she could possibly need. That surprised her. The unmarried men she'd known back in Ohio had taken most of their meals in cafes and restaurants.

She picked up a small jar containing a yellowish-brown powder. A scrap of paper was tied with a string around the jar but the string covered some of the penciled writing. With one finger, she adjusted the string so she could read what it said—cumin.

She'd never heard of such a thing. Was it a medicine? Tea? What?

While she was pondering this mysterious powder, she heard the front door close and Pete's footsteps on the stairs leading up to the second floor. She put the jar back on the shelf, noticing a few other small jars with similar pieces of paper attached to them. She didn't want to keep Pete waiting by taking the time to study the jars, so she left the kitchen, climbing the stairs to join him.

When she reached the top of the stairs, she found four rooms opening from a central area covered with a thick rug. A sound came from one of the rooms, so she approached it, pausing at the doorway.

Heat rose in Kathryn's cheeks when her gaze landed on the four-poster bed against one wall. It was much larger than her bed at home, its size seeming to fill the room. In a way, it made sense. She couldn't imagine Pete sleeping in her bed back in Ohio without his feet hanging off the end.

A log-cabin patterned quilt in shades of green and gold covered the bed. A bureau with a jug and basin on top stood on the opposite wall. Beside it was an intricately carved writing desk. A standing mirror stood in the corner. Thick dark green curtains hung at a large window.

The room suited him—masculine. Where she'd be at his mercy.

"This is our room."

Pete's voice burst into her thoughts. She spun around to face him. "I…I assumed as much…"

"You're welcome to change whatever you like in the house, but I'd appreciate it if you wouldn't make our bedroom all frilly." Worry lines creased his forehead.

If she wasn't so tense, she would have made a joke, but she wasn't feeling very light-hearted at the moment. "I won't," she agreed. "I promise I'll leave it just as it is."

He shot a smile at her that made her knees weak. "I'll go get the horses bedded down. Shouldn't take me too long, but long enough that you can do whatever you need to."

Without waiting for her to say anything, he turned and left. His heavy footsteps faded and the front door clicked shut. Kathryn sagged to the side of the bed, her hands twisting in her lap.

She sucked in deep, calming breaths, willing her heart to stop racing and her hands to stop trembling long enough that she could undress and slip into the pale blue flannel nightgown she'd packed for tonight.

She was tying a blue ribbon to the braid she'd made in her hair when she heard his footsteps on the stairs. Her heart fluttered inside her chest when he came into the room.

"I forgot to bring this in," he said, putting her carpetbag on the bed. "I hope you didn't need anything in there."

She shook her head, her throat tight.

"You're really beautiful, you know that?" he said softly, closing the gap between them.

Kathryn's eyes burned. She'd never been told she was beautiful before, and his words touched her deeply. She didn't know how to respond, so she lowered her gaze.

He hooked a finger under her chin and brought

her head up so he could see her face. "I get the impression you haven't been told that a lot by a man."

"No," she replied. "I haven't really even had a suitor. There was never time, and my father chased away any man who might have been interested."

During their ride from the train station to Sapphire Springs, she'd told him about her life in Ohio, about her father and what had driven her away.

"Remind me to thank your father one day for keeping you for me," he said.

She blushed again.

"Look, Kathryn, I want us to be honest with each other right from the start, and I want us to be able to talk to each other about anything and everything."

She wasn't sure what was coming, but she wanted to be able to be honest with her husband, too. The only person she'd been able to really talk to had been Charlotte, and now she was hundreds of miles away. They would write letters, but that wasn't the same. If she could talk to Pete the way she had to Charlotte… She smiled sweetly. "I'd like that too."

"There's something I need to tell you, and I likely should have told you before I asked you to come all the way out here, but I was worried you'd change your mind."

A chill washed over her and a knot formed in her stomach. Was he a drunkard? Worse? A criminal? "What is it?" she choked out.

"I expect you're hoping that once we get to know each other, we'll fall in love."

That was exactly what she'd hoped for, but she was getting the impression that love wasn't something he was interested in. He wanted honesty, but she couldn't shame herself enough to tell him she'd traveled to Texas hoping that she'd find true love.

She shrugged. "I came because staying in Ohio wasn't an option." At least that much was true.

"Good. I'm glad you're here, and I expect I'll grow to have feelings for you and I hope you'll feel the same way about me, but I know I won't ever love a woman the way a husband should love his wife."

Kathryn's hopes for the future plummeted. She hadn't imagined her husband would fall in love with her at first sight, but to be told point blank that he'd never love her…

She wouldn't dwell on that now. Instead, she raised her gaze to meet his head-on. What she saw in his eyes was sadness and resignation. What had happened to him to make him reject love?

"That's a shame," she said softly, "because from what I've seen, love between a husband and a wife can be a glorious thing."

He jammed his hands in his pockets and looked away.

She waited, wondering what else he could possibly have to say. Finally, he looked back at her. "That might be true, but it won't happen for me. I'm not capable of really loving a woman."

Her heart ached for him. How sad for him to live his life feeling that love wasn't possible.

"Look," he went on, "I know we don't know each other, and it is our wedding night…"

Again, her face burned and her heart raced so much she was afraid it might explode. He planned to exert his rights when he'd just rejected any possibility of love between them?

"I don't want to live with you like you're my sister," he said. "Do you know what I mean?"

She did. Her throat tightened until she could barely breathe and speaking was impossible. Not that she knew what to say anyway.

She nodded, but he didn't go on. Finally, she managed to swallow past the dryness in her throat and croaked out a few words. No matter that he'd just told her he'd never love her, she knew her duty. "It's your right…"

"Just because something is my right doesn't make it right," he countered. "I wanted you to know how I feel, but I've never forced a woman into my bed yet, and I don't intend to start now."

Kathryn couldn't do anything but stare, her mind whirling. Was he really willing to wait for her?

"You look like you're going to your execution," he added.

"I admit I'm a little afraid. I've never done… that…" she croaked out, lowering her head to hide her cheeks that were burning with embarrassment over even talking about such things. And he was so big…

"I figured that by your reaction when I kissed you

after the wedding, and I'm glad. So, while I'd like us to share the bed, we'll wait until we get to know each other better and you're more comfortable with the idea before we do anything else."

"We will?"

"We will, unless you want to do more," he said. "I'll leave it up to you whenever you're ready."

She'd expected him to be forceful, taking charge, demanding his rights. From what Charlotte had told her, men had needs, and if their wives didn't take care of those needs, they would find other ways.

Kathryn wasn't quite sure how to deal with his offer to wait. Not that she didn't appreciate it. But she did have her limits. "I…thank you for being so understanding, but I'll tell you now, I won't stand for you frequenting brothels—"

His brows arched and he laughed, the sound echoing off the walls. "A brothel? You think I'm going to go to a soiled dove?"

Oh, heavens! This whole conversation was so uncomfortable…but he'd told her they should be honest with each other. If she didn't make her position clear now, she couldn't very well complain later.

Swallowing down her embarrassment, she met his gaze. "I've been told men have…needs."

A twinkle appeared in his eye, and she got the impression he was enjoying her discomfort just a little. "That we do. But were you told that women also have needs?"

Her eyes widened and she gasped. "No. That's

impossible. What you're talking about…I mean, what I think you're talking about, it's a woman's duty. Not for pleasure."

"That's where you're wrong," he contradicted with a chuckle. "And one day, I'll remind you that you thought pleasure was impossible. There is one thing, though."

"What's that?"

"So that I don't get the wrong idea, when the time comes and you're ready, I want you to say the words. Do you understand what I'm telling you?"

"What words?"

"You'll have to tell me straight out that you want to make our marriage real."

Her mind whirled. She had to admit she'd liked the sensations that had rushed through her when he'd kissed her—brief as it was—after their wedding. She couldn't help wondering how it would feel to be kissed properly, the way she'd seen Owen kiss Charlotte once when she'd come across them unexpectedly in the garden one evening before they were married.

But the rest …

Her cheeks flamed. "This conversation is—"

"For another time," he said. "Not tonight. You've had a long trip, and tomorrow will be here before we know it. Now get under the covers before you catch cold."

She slid into bed, rolling to her side so her back was to him. She heard him kick off his boots and undress, and then the mattress dipped when he climbed in beside her.

"Kathryn?"

"Yes?" she answered.

"I promise I won't do anything else, but I really would like to be able to kiss you when we go to bed at night. Would that be all right?"

Her breath hitched in her throat. She rolled over. He was lying on his side, propped up on one elbow. His chest was bare, his muscles tense beneath his skin. Something deep inside her heated.

Her heartbeat fluttered. She nodded shyly.

He shifted, loomed over her, bracing his weight on his other arm until she was trapped. Then he lowered his head toward her.

His mouth touched hers, gently grazing her lips. She forgot to breathe. Her entire body tingled as his kiss deepened and she found herself wanting to be closer, to feel his body against hers. Her arms slid around his waist and drew him closer, her breasts pressed against the hard muscles of his chest. She thought she heard a tiny moan. Was that her? She didn't know. All she knew was that she never wanted this to end.

Then he released her, and she felt…empty. She'd never experienced such sensations and emotions.

He gazed down at her, his breathing ragged. "Goodnight," he said softly as he rolled away from her and turned off the lamp. "Sleep well."

Kathryn woke the next morning to the sound of birds chirping outside and sunlight streaming through a gap in the thick curtains at the window. The aroma of frying bacon reached her nose.

She tugged the quilt around her and as she rolled over, her gaze landed on the dresser where Pete had put their marriage license. Then she remembered.

She was a married woman now. And by the smells drifting through the open door, her husband was cooking breakfast.

How late was it? She couldn't remember ever sleeping much past sunrise. What would Pete think of her, lazing in bed while he had to make his own meals?

She bounded out of bed. The room was already warm, but she quickly dressed in the suit she'd worn the day before. She'd have time to unpack and find something cooler to wear once he left the house. After she ran a brush through her hair, she pinned it into a knot at the nape of her neck.

When she entered the kitchen, Pete looked up from the bread he was slicing and smiled. "Good morning," he said. "How did you sleep?"

"Very well," she replied, heat stealing into her cheeks. In the daylight, she was embarrassed by how she'd responded to his kiss the night before. It had aroused something in her she'd never even known she possessed.

To cover her discomfort, she quickly crossed the room and plucked the spatula up off the counter. "I'll finish breakfast," she said, flipping the bacon so it didn't burn in the skillet.

"You don't have to——"

"I know by the supplies you have on hand that you're used to cooking for yourself, but I'm your wife now. I'll take care of you and the house."

Pete grinned, backing up a step as he threw his hands up in mock surrender. "Fine, but in all honesty, I'm a terrible cook."

"Yet your cupboards are well stocked, even down to something called cumin that I've never heard of before."

He chuckled. "I could tell you I know what it is, but I'd be lying. All I know is it's some kind of spice. I had a housekeeper until last fall. Her name was Consuela and she was from Mexico. She used all kinds of ingredients I'd never heard of."

"What happened to her?"

"She got married."

"Does she still live in town?" Kathryn asked. "I'd love to speak to her and find out how to use the spices she left."

A thought niggled at her. Was she just a replacement housekeeper? Had she just gone from running after her father night and day to running after another man?

It was possible, but after all, what married woman didn't spend her days cooking and cleaning for a man. At least now, it would be in her own home.

"No, she moved to a town up near Fort Worth somewhere. I've never used half what's on those shelves," he said. "I can manage eggs, and stew, but even those aren't very good, so I either have bread and cheese or jelly, and I eat most of my suppers at John's diner. He feeds me in exchange for the vegetables, eggs and milk I give him."

"Who's John?"

"He's my best friend. He owns the diner in town. I'll take you to meet him and his wife, Miranda, one day soon. Miranda came here as a mail-order bride and married John. I asked her to help me find a bride. She's the one who put the ad in the newspaper for me."

"I'm looking forward to meeting her then, to thank her. Now if you'll tell me where to find the eggs…"

"They're in the basket over there," he said,

pointing to a wire basket almost hidden behind a stack of dirty dishes. At least he had washed enough dishes and silverware that they could have their meal, she noticed.

A short time later, Kathryn set a plate of bacon, fried eggs and bread in front of Pete at the table. She filled her own plate and then poured them both coffee he'd brewed.

She sat opposite him and took a sip. It was strong, but tasty. "Mmm," she murmured. "You might not be able to cook, but you do make a good pot of coffee."

"Thanks," he replied. "It's one of the few things I can do in the kitchen. These eggs are perfect. Usually mine are either hard-cooked or raw. Can't ever get them right."

Kathryn chuckled. "Well, now you don't have to worry. I do know how to make eggs."

"When we're finished here, how about I show you around the farm? It was too late to show you everything last night."

"I'd like that."

Pete drained his coffee. "I've been busier than usual over the winter," he said. "A couple even came from over Austin way a little while ago to ask me to build a bed, dresser and wardrobe for their new house."

"I'm not surprised." Kathryn got up and began to clear the table. "Your work is beautiful."

Pride swelled in her chest. Her husband was not only handsome and kind, he was talented, too.

He must have faults, though. She knew that. Everyone did. She only hoped that Pete's weren't so unbearable that she'd regret her decision.

Pete held Kathryn's hand as he ushered her outside a short time later. When they got to the bottom of the steps, Kathryn pulled her hand away from him and took a few steps into the yard before turning around and getting a good look at the house for the first time. It wasn't at all like the large brick house she'd grown up in, and she was happy about that. That house had always seemed more like one of the office buildings in the middle of the city than a home.

She smiled. The house looked much bigger in the daylight and had a fresh coat of white paint, with dark blue shutters and front door. Three rocking chairs took up the front porch, with small tables between them. She wondered how often Pete had time to sit on the porch and enjoy the fresh air and view.

Weeds grew thick between the pink flowers in the small border garden along the porch. She hoped she'd have time soon to get rid of them and add more plants, maybe even a rosebush or two if they'd grow in this climate. One day, maybe Pete would even build a white picket fence around the house. She'd always wanted to live in a house with a white picket fence.

"Come on around back." Pete came to stand

beside her and took her hand again. "Let me show you what I've planted in the vegetable garden."

"Already? The ground is still too hard in Ohio," she told him.

"We can plant much earlier here."

"I do want to see your garden," she said, looking up and giving him a smile, "but first, can I see your workshop?"

Pete's brows lifted in surprise. "My workshop?"

She nodded. The question in his voice made her wonder if she'd said something wrong. "Do you not build your furniture in your workshop ?"

He laughed. "I do," he said. "I suppose it could be called a workshop, but I've never thought of it as anything more than a big shed."

"Oh," she said, joining him in a chuckle. "It is where you work, so that makes it a workshop."

"That's true, and it does sound nicer than a shed."

She laughed again.

"I'm surprised you want to see it. I thought you'd be more interested in the garden than in my shed."

"To be honest," she replied. "I thought I would be, too, but seeing the beautiful furniture you've built in the house, I'm curious to see what else you're working on."

"I work on more than one thing at a time. Right now, I'm working on a few smaller things, but most of the time, I'm working on the bedroom furniture for the folks in Austin. It's my biggest project yet," he said as he led her across the grass toward the weathered building he called a shed.

Pete opened the door to the shed, the familiar scents of cut wood and lacquer filling his nose. Dust motes hung in the shaft of sunlight coming through the window.

The shed was large, almost as big as the barn, and filled with lumber, tools and half-finished projects. A workbench stretched the length of one side, and two sawhorses stood near the door. Sawdust, nails and scraps of wood littered the floor.

The whole shed was a mess. A giant mess. He'd never expected Kathryn to want to see the shed. No other woman he'd known had been interested in his work, so it had never occurred to him that Kathryn would ask to see it.

He stood aside. Kathryn brushed against him as she went inside and his senses heightened. He might not love this new wife of his, but he did like her more than he'd expected to.

"Oh," she gasped, rushing across to a cradle he was making as a gift. He'd taken even more pains than usual with the cradle, and it was turning out better than he'd hoped.

"It's beautiful," Kathryn exclaimed, running her fingers over the dark wood. He'd carved flowers and vines into the sides. All that was left to do now was to lacquer it.

"It's a gift for a friend and his wife who are having their first child soon," he told her. "I hope they like it."

"They must be good friends," she commented.

"They are."

"Didn't you say your furniture supports you?" she asked.

He nodded. "It does, but I don't need much money. It'll support both of us."

"City people would pay a lot of money for this kind of workmanship."

Pete shrugged. "I'm already busier than I'd like to be, but the orders came in before Miranda put the ad in the newspaper. I didn't really think anyone would answer the ad, and I sure didn't expect to be married by now."

"You didn't? Why not?"

He shrugged. Maybe because he'd been blunt about what he was looking for. Maybe because he hadn't mentioned romance, or love. Maybe…

"Your advertisement was open and honest, not filled with flowery words and promises that are easily broken."

"I'm glad you thought so and that you wrote back." The ad had brought Kathryn to him, and the more he learned about her, the more he was growing to like her. He'd only known her for one day, but already she seemed to be the kind of woman he could grow to like very much. That was all he hoped for, a woman he could spend his life with that wouldn't bore him or make him want to run for the hills.

"I'm so busy right now, I won't be able to spend as much time with you as I'd like to, but once these are finished, I'll cut back if we can manage without me working so much."

"That would be nice," she admitted. She wanted to spend more time with him, to get to know him better and maybe…maybe one day he would realize he was wrong and that he could love a woman. Love her.

"Money doesn't really mean much to me, as long as I have enough to get by. Having a lot of money causes more problems than it solves."

Kathryn shot him a curious glance. "Do you really think so?"

He nodded. "A day sitting on the riverbank with a fishing pole in my hand. Spending time with friends. Listening to Amos playing his fiddle or reading a good book. Those are worth more than money to me. I'm happy with what I have."

Kathryn shook her head slightly, as if she couldn't believe what she was hearing. "I've never known anyone who wasn't obsessed with making more and more money."

Unease washed over him. Was money important to her? Was she like his mother, who'd spent every cent his father had brought home, and even racked up credit at the mercantile because she was never content with what she had?

She crossed to where he was standing just inside the door. "My family was well off, but whether they were happy or not, I don't know."

"See," he commented with a smile. "We both kept a little secret. You never mentioned that your family was rich. I can't give you luxuries. Do you think you can be happy with what I can provide?"

She nodded. "Money isn't important to me either," she said, "and it sounds as if we'll get along just fine."

A drop of suspicion poked at Pete's brain. Was she telling the truth? Did money mean nothing to her, or was she merely telling him what she thought he wanted to hear? He'd have to wait and see.

"I don't need much," he said. "And now, I hope that sitting on the porch in the evenings looking out over our land with you by my side and two or three kids sleeping upstairs will be one more thing I'll enjoy and be grateful for."

A flush rose in Kathryn's cheeks, and he smiled at her innocence. Strangely enough, he hadn't thought much about having children of his own until now. What would they look like? Little girls with Kathryn's daintiness and beauty, sons who he could teach to fish and work alongside him.

"I've always made enough to get by. I have a roof over my head and enough to eat. That's all I really needed until now. But you don't have to worry. I'll make sure you and any children we might have don't do without."

A flush crept into her cheeks, and he was beginning to see that any talk of what went on in the bedroom or the resulting children made her blush.

"I can't ask for more than that." She smiled at him, then turned away and wandered through the shed, stopping to pick up a tool or to look closely at some of the intricate carvings in the furniture that was in the process of being made.

She hadn't mentioned her family was wealthy in her letter. He hoped she'd still think the same way when she couldn't buy all the doodads and new fashions that came along.

"You are a very talented man," she announced, interrupting his thoughts as she crossed to where he was standing, her hips swaying gently, her skirt swishing in the sawdust on the floor.

For the first time he could remember, he blushed. His chest tightened with an emotion he'd never felt before. For some reason he couldn't explain even to himself, it pleased him that she thought highly of him and his work.

He wasn't sure he liked that.

Pete took Kathryn's hand and ushered her around the back of the house a short while later. She hadn't thought to look out the kitchen window that morning, and when she saw the garden, her eyes widened in surprise.

Rows of tilled soil seemed to go on until they reached a row of bushes and trees. He'd told her he grew vegetables, and shoots of new plants were showing through the dirt in some of the rows, but she had no idea what kind of vegetables they were. Other rows were nothing but mounds of dirt.

A few chickens pecked at the ground, scattering as Pete led her around the edge of the garden. "It's still early, but the cauliflower, lettuce and peas are almost ready. Next month, we'll have cabbage and carrots. I'll be planting onions soon, and then tomatoes and beans."

He pointed to the trees and bushes at the far end of the garden. "Wild blueberries, raspberries and strawberries grow over there, and I have a couple of apple trees as well."

"Oh," she exclaimed, "I can't wait to be able to cook whatever I want when I want. It's like having your own mercantile right in your yard."

He nodded and shot her a grin. "I hadn't thought about it, but I suppose it is."

"You grow a lot of vegetables for one man," she put in.

"It is too much for me, but like I told you, I give what I don't use to John and Miranda in exchange for meals, and what they don't need, I sell to the mercantile in town."

"I see."

He looked down at her, a frown forming. "What's wrong?"

She hadn't realized her tone had changed, but he must have sensed the concern in her voice. "I'm a little worried," she said. "Now that I'm here, we'll be using double what you used before. That'll cut your income in half."

"I won't have to eat at the diner every night so John will start paying me for what they need."

He reached out and clasped her shoulders, gently turning her to face him squarely. "Don't worry. If we can't manage on what we have now, I'll sell more of my work, that's all. It'll be fine."

She nodded in agreement, even though she wasn't sure at all. She'd have to make sure she was thrifty and there was no waste.

"I've already milked the cow and fed the hog and the chickens, so now I need to get to work. Can you manage in the house by yourself?"

Kathryn nodded. "Of course. I'm looking forward to taking care of it."

"And me, I hope," he said, giving her hand a squeeze.

Her face heated and she lowered her gaze, nodding slightly. "Yes," she murmured. "And you."

"I'm in the shed if you need me," he said, walking away.

Kathryn watched him until he disappeared inside his workshop, then stood for a few minutes surveying the fields around her and listening to the silence.

This was her home now, and Pete was her husband.

She liked him, and she thought he liked her. After all, if he didn't, why would he have asked to kiss her the night before?

Her insides tingled at the memory, and if she was being completely honest with herself, she was looking forward to another kiss at bedtime.

CHAPTER 6

"Do you need anything at the mercantile?" Pete asked one morning when Kathryn had been in Sapphire Springs for a little more than a week. "I'm going into town to pick up lumber at the mill. You haven't taken time to even see the town yet."

He was right. She hadn't spared a minute for herself since she'd arrived, but the results were worth all her hard work. She hadn't had time yet to clean the windows or to take the rugs outside and beat them on the clothesline, but the inside of the house was clean, the laundry was done, and she'd rearranged the kitchen cabinets.

Twice, she'd fed the chickens, and she'd told Pete that once the house was in order, she'd take over that chore for him. She'd definitely leave the egg-gathering to him, though. Those chickens were ornery, as she'd found out the hard way the first time she'd gone into the chicken coop.

"I do need flour," she told him, "and I would like to get some cocoa if you don't mind. There's a recipe for chocolate cake I want to try."

"Chocolate cake?"

She nodded. "Do you like it?"

"I do, but the way you're feeding me, I'm going to be so fat you're going to have to stop cooking and start sewing me new pants and shirts."

"I enjoy cooking for someone who appreciates it. And…" She paused, not sure how to ask what she wanted to. "Well, would you mind if I invite Miranda and Audra to lunch one day?"

At church the Sunday before, John had introduced her to Miranda and Audra, the other mail-order bride who'd come to Sapphire Springs to marry a rancher. She'd immediately felt comfortable with them, which was something she'd always struggled with back in Ohio. She'd found it difficult to make friends, although she couldn't say why. Sensing that she, Miranda and Audra would become good friends in time helped to ease the bouts of homesickness she'd experienced lately.

It made no sense, really. She didn't miss her father's complaints and demands, but she missed him anyway. And she missed Charlotte so much. Forming friendships with the other women in town would help to make her feel less alone.

Not that Pete didn't do his best to keep her company, but having women friends was different. She'd tried once to explain it to him, but he hadn't understood. She wondered if maybe men didn't feel the need for close friendships the way women did.

"You don't need to ask my permission to invite someone here," he told her. "This is your house as much as mine now. And I'm happy to sample any recipes you want to experiment with," he added with a grin. "Now, what time will you be ready to go?"

"A few minutes," she said.

"Good. I'll go hitch the team and meet you outside."

Kathryn hummed as she hung up her apron and pinned her hat on her hair. Pete might not love her, but at least he liked her. Maybe one day he'd care about her as much as she was beginning to care about him.

"Do you like this one?" Pete's voice drifted into Kathryn's mind as she studied the selection of kitchen utensils in the mercantile later that day. The ladle she'd been using was beginning to rust, and he'd agreed when she'd suggested buying a new one the day before.

She hadn't been paying attention, and didn't hear what he'd said. Turning toward him, her eyes widened when she saw the bolt of crimson, brown and bright yellow fabric he was holding.

"What do you think of this for a new dress?" he asked. "It's bright and—"

"Heavens, no," she replied with a laugh. Everyone in town would see her coming for miles if she made a dress out of the fabric he was showing her. She couldn't imagine what anyone would use the gaudy material for, but she was sure every woman she knew would never be seen wearing a dress made out of it. "But I don't need a new dress anyway. There's nothing wrong with the dresses I have."

"You need cotton dresses here," he pointed out. "I've seen the sweat dripping off the end of your nose when you're cleaning, and it's not even the middle of summer yet. It's going to get a lot hotter than what it is now, and I don't want you fainting from the heat."

She crossed to where he was standing in front of a shelf filled with bolts of fabric—cotton, linen and wool, as well as fabrics she didn't recognize. "First of all, women don't sweat," she said, her voice little more than a whisper in case anyone heard them talking about something so personal. "And second, I've never fainted in my life."

"Well, there's a first time for everything," he pointed out. "And whatever you want to call sweating, we all do it. I can take my shirt off if I get too warm when I'm working, but you can't, so if you won't buy a dress or some material to make yourself one or two, I'll buy it for you and get someone else to make it."

"I—"

He grinned, a twinkle appearing in his eyes. "And it looks like you don't think much of my fashion taste."

She couldn't decide whether he'd seriously chosen that fabric or whether he was teasing her, but she couldn't take the chance he'd really buy it. "Fine," she said with an exasperated sigh.

For the next few minutes, she examined the different fabrics, finally deciding on a length of pale green fabric with white rosebuds.

"You need more than one dress."

"This will do for now." She tugged the bolt out of the pile. "I'll get another one next time."

"Make sure you do, or I'll get one for you," he reminded her. "And I don't think you'd like my choice."

She laughed and made her way toward the counter.

The clerk was taking care of another customer, so she wandered through the store until a flash of something caught her eye. She moved closer.

The sunlight had struck a silver tea service on a counter near the back of the store. She stopped to look closely at it. Her fingers grazed the flower-and-fern engravings on the gleaming teapot. A wave of melancholy washed over her.

"What are you looking at?" Pete's voice shattered the memories flooding her mind.

She looked up at him, blinking back the tears that threatened. "It's beautiful, isn't it?"

He shrugged. "I suppose so, but I can't see anybody in town except maybe the mayor having any use for something like that."

"My mother had a tea service just like it," Kathryn said quietly. "She served tea from it every afternoon. When I was younger, I felt so grown-up and special when I had tea poured from a silver teapot."

She turned toward the clerk, and noticing that the customer was gone, asked, "How much is this?"

"Well," the clerk replied, "a customer ordered it all the way from New York but he died before it got here, so I can let you have it for fifteen dollars."

"That's very reasonable."

She saw Pete's brows arch, but he didn't make any comment.

"I'll just take this today," she said, crossing the store and setting the bolt of fabric on the counter. "And five pounds of flour, a half-pound of cocoa and two pounds of sugar, please."

"How's married life?" Duncan McTavish, the owner of the sawmill, wiped his forehead with the sleeve of his shirt and scrubbed at his bushy ginger beard. "The little lady ready to run for the hills yet?"

"Not yet," Pete replied. Maybe soon, though, he added to himself. The way she'd looked at that teapot... She wanted it. He could see it in her eyes, in the way she fondled it, running her fingers across the design.

Then she'd told him her mother had had one just

like it, and she'd thought fifteen dollars wasn't expensive. Did she expect him to buy it for her? Hell, fifteen dollars was a lot of money for something just to pour tea out of, silver or not. He could buy enough kerosene to last them a year for less than that. The china teapot on the top shelf of the cabinet in the kitchen did the same job, and it had cost him less than a dollar.

There was no way he could afford to spend that kind of money to buy the silver teapot for her, even if he wanted to. Was she starting to change, to miss the luxuries she had back in Ohio? If he asked her, she'd likely deny it, but it sure looked like she was starting to regret coming to Texas.

"Your order's ready," Duncan said, drawing his attention back to the stack of lumber on the platform outside the mill. He'd built it a few months ago so that it was the same height as the back of the wagons. It made loading so much quicker and easier that Pete often wondered why he'd never seen another sawmill with one.

"I'll give you a hand to load it into the wagon if you're ready to go," Duncan added, handing Pete the bill.

"I am."

Fifteen minutes later, the slabs of wood were tied into the wagon. He paid Duncan, waved goodbye and climbed into the seat where Kathryn was waiting.

He was tempted to ask her if she was beginning to wish she hadn't come to Texas, but a tightening in his chest stopped him. He realized he was afraid he wouldn't like her answer.

Days stretched into weeks and every day she spent with Pete made her like him a little more. Each day, she looked forward to their quiet evenings sitting on the porch, or their battles over a game of cribbage using a board Pete had made out of mahogany and boxwood inlaid with mother-of-pearl diamonds.

And, she admitted much to her own chagrin, she looked forward to their kisses. Every night when they got into bed, he'd turn to her, slide an arm behind her back and pull her close. Then he'd kiss her with an urgency that sent her senses reeling. He'd press against her and it was plain he wanted more than what she'd agreed to.

She wanted more than a kiss, too. She wasn't sure exactly what it was she wanted, but she wanted more of something that would ease the ache she felt deep inside when he turned away from her and said good-night. She was far too shy to ask him what that ache could mean.

"Have you seen the gouge I was using a few days ago?" Pete's voice interrupted her thoughts.

She looked up from the bread she was kneading at the kitchen worktable, embarrassment flooding her as if he could read where her mind had been. "No," she replied shortly.

He moved closer, studying her face. "What's wrong? Are you sick?"

"No. I'm fine." She looked away, focused on the tree outside the window.

"You're flushed. Are you sure you don't have a fever? I can go get the doc—"

"Really, I'm fine." She lowered her gaze and punched the bread dough, forcing a lightness to her voice that she didn't feel. "Did you leave it in the bedroom? The barn? Or maybe out in the chicken coop?"

He gave her a wry grin. "Very funny."

"You do leave things in the strangest places sometimes," she pointed out. "Do I need to remind you of where I found your money clip last week?"

"No. But I'm sure I had the gouge in the shed. I was using it to carve out the roses on the dressing table I'm making for Mrs. McCarthy."

"It must be there somewhere." Kathryn returned to her kneading, then paused. She shot him a smile and shook her head.

"I'll keep looking."

She chuckled. "It's a good thing you can't take your brain out of your head and put it down somewhere. We'd be in a lot of trouble." She wiped her hands on her apron. "Would you like me to come and help you look for it?"

"No. I'll find it. Wouldn't want to ruin the bread," he said with a grin.

Kathryn shook her head as Pete left the kitchen.

She'd never known anyone to be so forgetful about where he left things. No matter what he was doing, whatever he was using would be left behind him when he was finished.

It seemed she spent the better part of her day picking up after him and putting things back in their rightful place. But, she reminded herself, if that was his worst fault, she was a lucky woman.

She'd just put the bread into the oven when she heard a noise coming from outside the back door. She listened, and the sound stopped. Assuming Pete was doing something, she ignored it for a few minutes. Then she heard it again, a soft sound that almost sounded like whimpering.

Looking out the window, she craned her neck but didn't see anything unusual.

This wasn't a city. Pete had warned her about the wildlife here—coyotes and wolves being the most dangerous.

It might not be wise to go outside to find out the source of the sound, but her natural curiosity won. She looked around for a weapon, just in case. Through the open doorway, she noticed Pete's rifle standing in the corner behind the front door. She considered it for a few seconds, then decided against it. She'd never shot a gun of any kind, so she'd be more likely to hurt or kill herself than anything else.

An empty skillet sat on the stove. Not much protection, but it was the best she could do. Picking it up, she opened the door and stepped outside.

CHAPTER 7

Kathryn paused, listening.

A faint breeze whipped up dust and rustled the leaves of the oak tree that shaded the house. Then, she heard it again. This time, it sounded as if it was coming from under the porch stairs.

Skillet raised and ready, she crouched and peeked under the stairs. In the shadows, two brown eyes stared back at her. Her heart skipped a beat and she let out a squeak, jumped back and lost her balance, landing on her backside in the dirt.

The animal didn't attack. Didn't move.

Kathryn squinted, peered into the dark space under the stairs. Far back in the shadowy corner, a tail moved, and she realized the wild creature she was prepared to defend herself against was a dog. And beside the dog were four newborn puppies.

The dog gave her a guarded look, then nudged

the puppies away from her and moved so that she was between her babies and Kathryn.

Kathryn smiled gently at the way the dog had shifted to protect her young. It seemed it wasn't only human mothers who'd put themselves at risk for their children.

What should she do? She had no experience with birth of any kind. Women had midwives or at least other female friends or family. But animals? She had no idea.

Scrambling to her feet, she raced around the house and across the yard to Pete's workshop. By the time she reached the building, she was out of breath. "Pete! Pete!" she cried out as she threw open the door.

Pete dropped the hammer he was holding. "What's wrong?"

"A dog…at the back of the house…puppies…"

Closing the gap between them, Pete gripped her shoulders. "Calm down. What are you talking about?"

Between breaths, Kathryn explained what was happening under the stairs. "They'll be fine," Pete said after she was finished. "Animals have babies all the time without people interfering."

"We have to take them inside. They're so tiny—"

"We'll go take a look, but no, we have to leave them alone. The mama knows how to look after them."

"But who does the dog belong to? Surely her owner must be worried."

Pete shrugged. "I don't know," he said. "I haven't

seen a dog around here before. She might just be a stray who found a safe place to have her pups. I'll figure out what to do with them later, but right now—"

"What do you mean?" The words came out in a gasp. Her hands formed into fists, her eyes narrowed and her lips pressed into a thin line. She would not allow him to dispose of them the way—

"What?" Pete's voice burst into a memory, one she'd shoved into a back corner of her mind. "You're as white as snow."

"I will not stand by and let you kill them!" She couldn't prevent the disgust in the tone of her voice.

"Are you crazy? Why would I kill them?"

She gazed up at him, her eyes filling with tears. "You're not going to?"

"Of course not," he said. "What would give you an idea like that?"

"My father… When I was six years old, our cat, Fluffy, had kittens. Three of them. My father…" The memory rushed back. "He took them…drowned them…he told us they'd run away, but I saw him take them outside into the shed at the back of our property."

Suddenly, Pete's arms were around her, holding her, stroking her back. "I promise, I'm not going to hurt them. I only mean that once they're moving around, I'll need to find a way so they don't wander off and get lost."

"Oh…" Kathryn muttered. Now she was embarrassed that she'd thought he was the kind of man who'd kill defenseless animals, other than for food. "I thought—"

Pete gripped her shoulders and took a step back. Meeting her gaze, he smiled gently.

Her breath hitched. He really was so handsome.

"She'll be fine," he said, "so just leave them be and go finish whatever you were doing. I'll be done in another hour or so."

"Good," she replied. "I'll have supper on the table when you come in."

"What are you making?"

"Beef stew and—" Her eyes widened. "Oh, no, the bread!" She'd completely forgotten it was in the oven when she'd gone outside. It was likely burned by now and there wasn't time to make a new loaf.

She tugged her hand out of Pete's grip and ran up the stairs into the house.

Kathryn rolled over, her eyes heavy with sleep. The quilt beside her had been thrown back, and she reached out, the space where Pete slept feeling cold to her touch.

She sat up, peering into the dark to see if he was in the room. There was no light coming through the curtains at the window to tell her it was dawn, so where was he? It was too early to be out doing chores.

Pulling a wrapper on, she padded down the stairs

and looked in the kitchen. The house was empty. Where had he gone? And why? She shivered, but whether it was from the cool air in the house or the fear that was slowly enveloping her, she couldn't say.

The back door wasn't latched properly, so she looked outside. The moon was half-hidden behind the clouds, but gave her enough light to see Pete crouched beside the stairs. He looked up as she stepped onto the porch. "I didn't mean to wake you."

"You didn't," she assured him. "What are you doing out here?"

"Figured the mama would be hungry by now," he said. It was then she noticed a plate of scrambled eggs on the ground and a bowl filled with water beside it. A quilt she'd seen on the shelf in the closet earlier lay near the opening.

Kathryn's heart swelled. She'd obviously married one of the kindest men she'd ever met.

"How are they doing?" she asked, slowly coming down the stairs to join him. The ground was cold and her toes squelched in a patch of mud from the rainstorm they'd had the day before.

"They seem to be okay," he said. "The pups will feed from the mama but she'll need food and water. What else do we have to feed her?"

That he was concerned about an animal told Kathryn so much about his character. Her mother had always told her that men who treated animals badly wouldn't treat humans any better. If his concern for the dog and her puppies was any indication, he was a kind and caring man.

The puppies were squirming, pushing each other out of the way as they all tried to get as close to their mother as possible. The dog raised her head and met Kathryn's gaze with her sad brown eyes, and Kathryn's heart melted. "Oh, I want to take them all inside where it's warm…"

"She won't be happy if you try to touch them yet," Pete told her. "Give it a day or two and see how she reacts. If we keep feeding her, she'll know we don't mean her any harm."

Kathryn smiled at Pete, her heart opening a little more and letting this man in. How was it possible that some woman hadn't snatched him up long before now?

Getting up, Pete reached out his hand. "She won't come to eat while we're standing here, so we'd best go inside."

As if his suggestion brought it on, she shivered, her thin wrapper offering little protection against the cool night air. She took Pete's hand, feeling his warmth seep up her arm. As she stood facing him, her heartbeat did a little dance.

"Your hands are freezing," he commented.

She chuckled. "That's nothing compared to my feet. I think they've turned into blocks of ice."

The clouds shifted, the moonlight bathing the yard in a faint glow.

He laughed then. "Come on, then. Let's get you

inside before you freeze to death. As it is, you're liable to catch cold."

Wrapping his arm around her shoulder and hugging her to his side, he led her back into the house.

"Do you want me to heat some water so you can wash your feet?" he asked, gazing at the mud drying between her toes.

She shook her head. "It's all right. I'll just wash them in the water that I didn't use at supper. It's warm enough."

It wasn't any warmer than her feet, she noticed as she scrubbed them clean while Pete waited for her.

"I saw the quilt you left out there," she said a few minutes later as they climbed the stairs once he'd bolted the doors. "That was a sweet thing to do."

He shrugged. "It was nothing."

He might have thought it was nothing, but to Kathryn, it showed once again his kindness and consideration for others, even stray dogs.

She slid into bed, listening as Pete moved around the room in the darkness. A few moments later, she felt the mattress dip at the side of the bed. Her side.

Then the blanket moved and she felt his hands on one of her feet, his fingers and thumbs kneading it in slow circles.

Startled, she bounded up, her fists clutched around the blanket as she peered at his shadow. "What...what are you doing?"

"You said your feet were cold," he replied. "I'm warming them for you. You don't like it?"

The heat from his hands, and the gentle pressure of his fingers and thumbs on first one foot and then the other warmed more than her feet. There was something so soothing that it eased the tension out of her whole body. At the same time, his touch was doing strange things to her insides, making her wonder what the touch of those hands could do on other parts of her body.

He rubbed her ankles, his fingers stealing up her calves.

In the silence, she heard herself suck in a breath.

Suddenly, he stood up, the imprint of the heat off his hands still seared into her skin. "You'd better get some sleep," he said. A few seconds later, she felt his weight on the mattress on his side of the bed.

For what seemed like hours, she lay in the darkness, listening to his even breathing. How was she supposed to sleep when her body was aflame from his touch?

He should never have touched her. Sure, it was only her feet, but it was enough to give him dreams he shouldn't be having. How long could he stand sleeping beside her, breathing in her lavender scent, feeling her skin brush against him during the night without going crazy with need?

He wasn't used to living like a monk and he hadn't realized how hard it would be, especially when the woman he wanted more than he'd ever wanted anything in his life was lying right next to him.

A few times, when he'd been sure she was sleeping, he'd wrapped one of her curls around his finger, wishing he could bury his hands in her hair. Wishing she would turn to him and let him know it was time…

It wasn't just a physical need, either. Sure, that was part of it, but over the past few weeks, even though he'd been fighting against it, he found himself wanting to spend time with her, missing her when he was in the shed working, making excuses to go into the house just so he could talk to her for a few minutes.

And that irritated him. He wouldn't let himself be like his father. The man had been so besotted with his mother that he'd worked day and night to give her what she wanted. And it had never been enough.

He had to be honest, though. Other than his suspicion that she missed the luxuries she'd grown up with, Kathryn didn't seem to be anything like his mother. In fact, she went overboard trying to be practical, to make do when it wasn't necessary, to apologize when she spent money on anything that wasn't an absolute necessity.

She went out of her way to make sure he didn't work too hard, and had even asked him to teach her about gardening and taking care of the animals so he'd have more time to spend with her, either sitting on the porch or playing cards.

She cared about him. That much was obvious in everything she did, both during the day and even at night. But she still hadn't told him she was ready to make theirs a real marriage.

She responded to his kisses, so that was something, he supposed. But kisses weren't nearly enough. He wanted her, every inch of her. She had no idea how much she was torturing him when she slid her arms around him and her hands splayed against his bare back, moving against him, molding herself to him.

But he'd made a promise, and he wouldn't go back on it. He had no choice but to wait.

And hope.

CHAPTER 8

The days flew by, and Kathryn found she had time to help Pete in his workshop and tend the garden. She'd planted flowers along the front of the house and even added some herbs to the vegetable garden.

Some of the vegetables were almost ready to harvest, and she was looking forward to learning how to put them up for winter. Miranda had offered to come out to the farm once the beans were picked and teach her how to can them.

She'd also learned how to drive the wagon and often took the eggs to the diner so that Pete could spend more time in his workshop.

Kathryn opened the gate to the makeshift pen beside the stairs that Pete had built to protect the puppies from wandering off. She crouched beside the stairs and slid the plate of leftover stew along the dried ground toward Lucky, sprawled out on the ground while the puppies played beside her.

Pete had laughed at her when she'd named the dog Lucky. Then she'd explained that the dog had been very, very lucky to have decided to have her puppies under their porch.

"Here you go," she said. "I bet you're hungry."

Lucky wagged her tail, raising a cloud of dust. Kathryn grinned. They had no idea what kind of dog Lucky was, only that she was light-colored and had sad eyes. It didn't matter to Kathryn. Lucky had wound her way around Kathryn's heart that first night. The dog was still timid, but over the past week or so, Kathryn had been able to get close enough once or twice to pet her. She was convinced that given enough time and love, Lucky wouldn't cower under her touch the way she did now.

Kathryn moved away so Lucky wouldn't be afraid to come out from under the stairs. Reaching up onto the porch, she picked up the bowl of fresh water she'd left there.

"What are you doing?"

Pete's voice coming from behind startled her. She spun around, forgetting about the bowl of water in her hands. Water splashed out of the bowl. Pete jumped, trying to get out of the way. He wasn't fast enough.

Kathryn's eyes widened in horror as the water sprayed his shirt, his neck, his face. "Oh...I'm so sorry..."

Pete ran his hand across his face and flicked the water off his hand. He glanced down at the bowl. "Never realized how skittish you are," he said with a smile.

"I always have been startled easily," she said with a sigh. "When we were little, my sister used to get a lot of pleasure from scaring me half to death every chance she got. At least once we got older, she realized how cruel it was and she stopped."

"I'll keep that in mind and give you as much warning as I can when I'm coming close."

She chuckled. "Especially if I'm holding anything liquid," she pointed out, clutching the bottom of her apron and using it to wipe the water drops off his face.

His dark eyes bored into hers, and her breath hitched in her throat. For long moments, neither of them spoke.

Finally, he cleared his throat. "Looks like you need to go back and fill the water bowl again. What's left in there won't last the dogs any time at all."

"They're so adorable, aren't they?"

He nodded. "They are," he agreed, "but they're getting too big for that pen."

She hadn't thought of that, but he was right. The puppies were big enough now that they were eating scrambled eggs, and cow's milk thickened with gravy. Soon they'd be eating table food like Lucky was. "Can you make it bigger?"

Pete took the bowl out of her hand and set it on

the porch. He faced her, giving her a sympathetic look. "We can't keep them locked up forever," he said gently. "The puppies have almost stopped nursing, so they'll soon be ready to be on their own."

Kathryn's heart tightened. Did he plan to let them go? "What…? Can't we keep them?"

"We don't need five dogs," he pointed out.

"Please?" She couldn't bear the thought of them being left to take care of themselves.

He studied her for a few seconds and his gaze strayed to the puppies in the pen. They were falling all over each other, tugging on a piece of thick rope Pete had tied in a knot. Then he laughed. "We don't *need* five dogs, but it looks like we *have* five dogs."

Kathryn was so grateful that without even thinking about it, she threw her arms around his neck and planted a kiss on his lips. "Thank you!"

As soon as her mouth touched his, she realized what she'd done. How could she have been so brazen? She began to pull away, but his arms reached around her and drew her against him. Her embarrassment at being so forward faded, and she was swept away in his kiss.

One hand splayed across her back, while the other threaded itself into her hair. His kiss deepened, and his tongue traced the seam of her lips, encouraging her to open them to him. Her heartbeat skittered in her chest as his tongue slipped inside her mouth, tangling with hers. Her body tingled, and need surged through her.

Something felt strange, something tugging on her. She couldn't think, could only feel. She wished whatever it was pulling at her would stop, but it didn't. What was it?

She drew herself out of Pete's grasp, her breathing ragged, her heart racing. Their goodnight kisses were always romantic and sweet, but they'd never been so … intense, so passionate. This kiss had inflamed her insides to the extent that she hadn't wanted it to ever end.

Again, she felt a tug on her skirt. She looked down. One of the puppies was chewing on her hem through one of the slats of the pen.

Pete's gaze followed hers. The laugh she heard escaping his lips was contagious. "I think he's jealous that I got to kiss the pretty lady," he said.

"Oh…" Her face flamed at the compliment. She didn't know how to respond, so she ignored it and reached down to dislodge the puppy from her skirt. She picked him up and nuzzled him against her neck for a few seconds before she set him back inside the pen. "I'll go and get more water," she added, turning her attention back to Pete. "Are you finished working for the day?"

"No," he replied. "I came back to tell you John stopped by a few minutes ago and invited us to supper with them on Sunday. I told him we would. I hope you don't mind."

Kathryn grinned. "I don't mind at all. I haven't seen Miranda for more than a minute or two after church in three weeks, and I've never really even spoken to John at all. It'll be nice to get to know him."

"Good. Now I'd better get back to work. I won't be much longer."

"It looks like it's going to be a nice evening to sit on the porch after supper," she said.

He smiled at her, an expression in his eyes she'd never seen before. "Sounds like the perfect way to end the day," he said, then walked away.

She watched him disappear around the side of the house before she went inside. A perfect way to end the day, she repeated to herself, and an almost perfect life. She suspected she was falling in love with Pete, and a perfect life would mean he loved her, too.

But as he'd told her on their wedding night, that wasn't going to happen.

Pete cast a glance at Kathryn sitting beside him in the wagon on the way to the Weavers' house that Sunday. She really was pretty, and the changes in her appearance since she got there only made her even prettier than she'd been that day at the train station. Sunshine had tinted her skin just a little and had shown up the gold strands in her hair. Her eyes sparkled and she was rarely without a smile. He found he enjoyed listening to her humming while she worked and wondered how he'd managed to stand the quiet before she came into his life.

Miranda opened the front door of the two-story house around the corner from the diner as Pete drew the wagon to a stop outside the gate.

In the time she'd been in Sapphire Springs, Kathryn hadn't been to the Weaver home. She stopped as they made their way up the stone path to the porch and crouched beside a shrub bearing pink flowers. "Aren't these pretty?" she asked, looking up at Pete and squinting into the sunshine behind him. "Do you know what they are?"

Pete shook his head and grinned. "Pink?"

"So you don't know," she said with a laugh. "Remind me to ask Miranda what kind of flowers these are. If she has any cuttings, I'd love some for the flower bed in front of our porch."

Once inside, Pete and John retired to the parlor to talk, while Kathryn followed Miranda into the kitchen. "You have a lovely home, Miranda," she said. She noticed a pile of children's books on a desk in the corner. "Where are the children?"

"John's aunt has them for the night. It's amazing that we get along now after what we went through when I first got here." Miranda picked up a wooden spoon and began to stir the gravy in the pot on the stove. "Not that we'll ever be good friends," she added with a slight chuckle, "but that's fine."

"Can I do anything?" Kathryn asked.

"If you can start setting the table, that would be a big help," Miranda told her. "The dishes are in the sideboard in the dining room."

Kathryn headed toward the dining room. Pete looked away from John as she entered and gave her a smile that made her knees weak and her heart begin to flutter behind her ribs. As she set the table, she sensed Pete's gaze following her but she was afraid to turn her head to see if she was right.

Miranda carried the meat platter and bowls of vegetables and potatoes. John smiled at her, love shining in his eyes. Oh, Kathryn thought, how she wanted to see that same look in Pete's eyes. "Supper's ready."

Pete held the chair for Kathryn. His fingers grazed her arm. Heat sparked inside her, and she drew in a shaky breath. She jerked her head upward to look into his dark eyes. Had he felt it, too? The tiny quirk of his lips told her his touch hadn't been an accident, that he'd wanted to touch her. What did it mean? She was well aware that he was eager to consummate their marriage, but he'd never touched her this way in company. Did it mean he was starting to care for her more, or was it merely a man's need for physical contact?

She met his smile with one of her own. The only way she would find out was to let him know that she was ready to share his bed the way a real wife did. But could she bring herself to do that?

Tucking her stray thoughts away, Kathryn focused on the conversation as they ate their meal and Miranda served apple pie and whipped cream for dessert. "That was delicious, Miranda," she said, scraping up the last crumb off her plate.

Miranda beamed. "I'm glad you liked it. Now why don't we have coffee in the other room where it's more comfortable?"

Pete and John settled in the parlor while Kathryn and Miranda served the coffee. It was only when she gave Pete his cup that Kathryn noticed the piano. She crossed the room and lovingly ran her fingers over the keys. "It's beautiful," she said. "Fluted walnut, isn't it?"

"It is," John answered. "Do you play?"

Miranda nodded. "I used to. I did love it so," she said, her voice soft as the memories of the hours she'd spent lost in the music washed over her. "Sometimes, especially after my mother passed away, losing myself in the music was the only thing that brought me any happiness."

"Miranda plays a little," John put in. "She's been teaching the children."

"Was your piano like this one?" Pete asked.

Kathryn shook her head. "My parents had a grand piano. I have a feeling they bought it strictly to show their friends they could afford one, because neither of them knew how to play."

"How did you learn?"

"My sister and I were given lessons almost from the time we were old enough to reach the pedals," she replied. "I had to sit on the very edge of the bench and only the tips of my toes could reach, but Mother was determined we'd start as young as possible."

"Will you play for us?" John asked.

Kathryn glanced at Pete. His expression was closed, as if something serious was going on in his mind. Was he upset at something she'd done? She couldn't imagine what that could be, but his jovial mood of just a short time before had disappeared. "Perhaps another time," she said. "It's getting late and we really should go."

"Maybe you could teach me a thing or two," Miranda put in. "I can play, but I didn't have any formal lessons, so you're probably much more skilled than I am."

"I'm happy to help if I can. And you can teach me how to make the perfect pastry. Mine isn't nearly as flaky as yours."

"It's a deal."

Pete plucked his hat and Kathryn's thin shawl off the hook near the door and draped the shawl over her shoulders. A few minutes later, Kathryn said good-night, knowing she'd made at least one friend in Texas.

Night had fallen and the blistering heat of the day had cooled by the time Kathryn and Pete climbed into the wagon to drive back to the farm.

"You're awful quiet," Pete said, casting a sidelong

glance at Kathryn sitting beside him on the seat. Her face was in shadow, the only light from the full moon in the clear sky above.

"Tired, that's all," she replied.

"Missing your piano?"

"What?"

He felt her shift beside him. "Your piano," he repeated. "You never told me you had a piano back in Ohio."

He didn't even know what a grand piano was. The only pianos he'd ever seen were those in the saloons.

"Should I have?"

"Well…a piano isn't something most people have."

"Many people I knew in Ohio have them."

"Rich people."

She didn't answer. What else hadn't she told him about her life and her family back east? Every time he started to think maybe she could be happy with the life he could provide for her, something came up that reminded him where she came from, the luxuries she'd grown up with, and that he'd never be able to offer her a life like the one she'd left.

"Why does it matter what I had back home?"

"I saw the way you looked at it. You miss it, don't you?"

"I do miss playing, but—"

"I can't afford to buy you a piano, Kathryn."

"I didn't ask you to."

"But you'd like one, wouldn't you?"

Kathryn let out a loud sigh that Pete couldn't miss hearing. "I don't know what's gotten into you tonight," she said. "I do miss playing the piano, but I've never said I want one, and I hope I've never made you feel that I'm not content with what we do have."

He had to admit that was true. She hadn't said a word about having to fetch water from the well or having to use the outhouse, although she did make a point of leaving the door open when it wasn't occupied. And so far, she hadn't complained about the lack of entertainment in Sapphire Springs compared to what she must have been used to in the city.

Still, he couldn't help feeling that she was only trying to be polite by keeping her complaints to herself. It was only a matter of time before she started nagging. After all, he was pretty sure his mother hadn't been a shrew when his pa first married her either.

"I can't give you all the frills and fripperies you had before so if that's what you want, you should go back east—"

"You're being ridiculous, and I won't listen to this a minute more. I've never asked for frills and fripperies and if you insist on putting words in my mouth, you can talk to yourself." He felt the seat shift and saw her shadow move. She'd turned her back on him.

He glared at her in the darkness, then flicked the reins and whistled. The team picked up its pace.

So much for the romantic ride in the moonlight he'd planned on.

CHAPTER 9

Kathryn was at her wits' end. Since their argument three days before, they'd barely spoken to each other, and only when it was absolutely necessary. She didn't know what to do, how to convince him that she was telling the truth when she'd told him she didn't need silver tea services or pianos or anything else. She was happier than she'd ever been.

She did know she couldn't go on like this, and when he came in for lunch, she'd tell him as much. But first, she had to go into town and take eggs to the diner.

"Good morning, Miranda," Kathryn called into the kitchen of The Blue Sapphire later that morning. "I've brought you some eggs."

Miranda peeked through the opening between the kitchen and the dining room. "Kathryn! What a nice surprise! I expected Pete. I've just made tea and I still have a few Imperial cookies left that I made yesterday. Do you have time?"

"I do, and even though it isn't even lunch time yet, I'll never turn down your cookies," Kathryn answered with a laugh.

Kathryn carried the egg basket into the kitchen. While Miranda steeped a pot of tea and put a tray together with cups, sugar, milk and cookies, Kathryn transferred the eggs to a waiting bowl on the counter. Then Miranda carried the tray into the dining room and set it on a table near the window. Kathryn followed with the teapot and the empty egg basket that she put on the chair beside her.

"You don't seem like yourself this morning," Miranda noted. "Is everything all right?"

"I'm fine," Kathryn lied, plastering the brightest smile she could muster on her face.

Miranda frowned. "Are you sure?"

"I don't want to bother you with my problems," Kathryn said. "Back in Ohio, I would have talked to Charlotte, my sister, and asked her advice. I miss her so."

Miranda's gentle smile faded. "I understand. I miss my sister, too."

"Is she still living back east?" Kathryn knew that Miranda had originally come from Massachusetts.

"No," Miranda told her. "She passed away before I came to Texas."

"Oh…I'm sorry…"

"She was indirectly the reason I came to Texas,

but I like to think she was watching over me and sent me to the perfect man for me so I wouldn't be alone."

Kathryn nodded. "I'm sure you're right."

"And although we don't have our sisters close by now, I think we can be good friends."

Kathryn smiled. "We can."

Miranda reached over and patted her hand. "Now, please tell me what's wrong. What's Pete done?"

Kathryn's eyes widened. "How did you know?"

Miranda let out a short laugh. "It's almost always men."

"The trouble is," Kathryn said when she was finished telling Miranda about their argument, "I really think I love him. I've never been in love before so I'm not sure that's what it is, but I feel different when he's with me. When he kisses me goodnight, it makes my insides feel … warm and tingly. And I miss him when he isn't there. Except for the last few days, that is," she added with a wry smile.

Miranda refilled Kathryn's cup and set the teapot on the trivet on the table. "Sure sounds like love."

"I don't know how to make him see that I don't need fancy dresses or a piano or anything else. I just need him to love me back, but he won't. Not ever. He told me that the day we got married."

Miranda's brows arched. "He what? He actually told you he'd never love you?"

Kathryn nodded miserably.

"I'm so sorry," Miranda said. "In time …"

"How much time?" Kathryn asked. "How long should I wait, hoping he'll love me? I thought he was beginning to care for me, that maybe one day he would love me, but these past few days…it's plain to see he doesn't. I'm not sure I can be content to live my life knowing the man I love will never love me back."

Miranda squeezed Kathryn's hand in sympathy.

"Now I really have to get back," Kathryn said, getting up and slipping the handle of the empty egg basket over her arm. "Thank you for the tea and cookies. They were delicious. And thank you for listening."

Kathryn's thoughts were so focused on Pete that when she was driving the wagon through town a few minutes later she almost didn't hear the woman calling her name. "Mrs. Fallon!"

She drew the wagon to a halt in front of the post office. A gray-haired woman she recognized as the postmistress hurried down the steps, waving an envelope. "I was just going to come over to the diner and give this to you," she said. The postmistress—Kathryn couldn't remember her name…Sue Ann? Susan? Suzanna?—handed her the envelope.

Kathryn grinned when she saw the precise penmanship on the front. She couldn't wait to get home and catch up on Charlotte's news.

Pete hammered the lid down on the tin of lacquer a lot harder than he needed to.

This couldn't go on. The past three days had felt like a lifetime, and even though he had trouble admitting it, their argument had been because he'd been a horse's behind.

He was tired of eating his meals in tense silence, of never seeing Kathryn smile or hearing the sound of her voice as she hummed while she worked. The nights were the worst. She found excuses to avoid him, and by the time he undressed and slid into bed beside her, she was asleep. Or pretended to be.

The more he thought about it, the more he realized he'd been wrong to jump to the conclusion that she missed the wealth she'd left behind.

Maybe she wasn't like his mother after all. Maybe she was more like Miranda and Audra and the other women he knew who seemed to be content with the life they had.

It wasn't as if she'd given him reason to think the way he did. She'd never once complained about not having enough, and when he really thought about it, she was more frugal than he was most of the time, assuring him she could make do with what she had rather than spend money on something new.

He swore to himself. They were living in the same house, but they might as well be miles apart. And he missed her.

He heard a wagon and looked out the window to see Kathryn drawing the team to a stop in front of the house. He smiled to himself as she quickly climbed down and hurried inside. He wanted to go to her, but he couldn't leave the lacquering of the chest he was working on half done. He'd take the rest of the day off to spend the time with Kathryn and try to make amends once he was finished putting on this coat of lacquer. Another half hour or so wouldn't make much difference.

As soon as he'd cleaned the brushes, he washed his hands at the basin outside and hurried into the house.

And found Kathryn sitting at the kitchen table, tears rolling unheeded down her face, a crumpled piece of paper in her hands.

Kathryn's world had crashed down on her. She could barely breathe. Her eyes stung and her throat ached. The words in the letter were blurred, but she didn't need to read them again. They were burned into her brain—words she'd never forget.

She felt Pete crouching beside her chair and his arms wrapping around her.

"What's wrong?" he asked.

His voice seemed to be coming from miles away. She gazed up at him, her vision clouded by her tears. "Papa..."

"Your father? Has something happened?"

"Papa...was killed...and Owen..."

Saying the words out loud made it even more real, and she couldn't contain the heartbreaking grief crushing her.

"What happened?"

"A…a carriage accident…on their way home from a meeting at church." She let out a whimper. "Oh…poor Charlotte…and the children…"

Pete tightened his hold on her, gently rubbing her back as she molded herself to him and let her tears flow until she was spent.

Finally, she raised her head and met his sympathetic gaze. She swallowed past the painful lump in her throat. "I thought…I hoped…"

"What?"

"The first letter I got from Charlotte after I left… she said Papa was angry, that I'd deserted him…and that I was no longer his daughter."

"Why didn't you tell me about that?" Pete asked. She must have been devastated, but she'd hidden it behind her smiles and singing. His sympathy for Kathryn slowly changed to anger with the man who'd caused her such pain.

"I knew I'd done the right thing, and the next letters Charlotte wrote, she said his health had improved and he was starting to go out again and spend time with his friends."

"You did what was best for him then," Pete reminded her.

She nodded and sniffled, blinking back more

tears. "I…did…and I hoped that one day…he'd forgive me. Now…"

Pete couldn't resist. He kissed her, a soft gentle kiss. "He would have."

"I'll never know."

"You have to believe that in time, he would have."

A sudden realization made her gasp. "It's my fault," she cried out. "Oh, Papa…"

"This is not your fault," he said sternly, cupping her chin and forcing her to look at him. "How could this be your fault?"

She took in a shuddery breath. "Don't you see? If I hadn't left…if I hadn't abandoned him… he wouldn't have gone out…he wouldn't have been there…"

Guilt squeezed her until she was sure she was going to be sick. Struggling out of Pete's grasp, she ran outside.

When she was finished, she looked up to see Pete waiting at the door. "I'll make you some tea," he said quietly.

She shook her head and came back inside. "I need to be alone for a little while. Do you understand?"

"I do," he answered. "I do."

Pete watched her trudge up the stairs to their bedroom, her head bowed, tears drying on her cheeks.

His insides ached with the need to take away her pain, but he knew from losing his own parents, even though his father didn't die, that nothing he could say would ease her grief. All he could do was to be there, to offer her his shoulder to cry on, his ear to listen if she needed to talk, and his arms to hold her when she needed comfort. Time would ease the overwhelming sadness she was feeling right now, but he wouldn't ever tell her there would be a place in her heart that wasn't quite whole again.

He still hadn't apologized for his tantrum—and that's what it had been—the night they'd had supper with the Weavers. Right now, though, that was the last thing on her mind. There would be a time to tell her how sorry he was, but first he had to help her deal with her grief.

He filled the kettle with water and put it on the stove to boil. She'd said she didn't want tea, but in a while, if she changed her mind, the water wouldn't take long to heat.

Sliding into the chair she'd vacated, he picked up the crumpled letter and skimmed it. When he got to the last paragraph, his chest tightened, and his muscles tensed.

"You have to come home," her sister had written. "I haven't officially met with Papa's attorney yet, but he did tell me that if you don't come back to Dayton and live here, your inheritance will go to Uncle Harry. Papa would roll over in his grave if that happened.

Please come back, not just for the money, but because I need you."

Pete had no idea who Uncle Harry was, but it was plain to see that whoever he was, her father wasn't on good terms with him.

Kathryn hadn't said anything about going back to Ohio. She also hadn't mentioned that her sister needed her.

He swore. Somehow, she'd torn down the walls he'd built around his heart and he'd fallen in love with her. He loved her smile, her kindness, her willingness to help in whatever way she could. He loved everything about her, right down to the way she puffed out little snores in the middle of the night to the squeaky sound she made when she tried to hum a high note.

How could this have happened? He'd sworn he'd never let himself fall in love. Would never let a woman have the kind of power over him that his mother had had over his father.

But it had. He loved her. And now, he was going to be miserable until she came home. If she came home.

Sure, they'd had an argument, but every married couple argued, didn't they? That didn't mean the marriage was over. Then again, most marriages weren't like theirs. Now she'd have enough money to live the way she always had. She could buy that silver teapot. And a piano. And anything else she wanted.

She'd told him money wasn't important to her, so she wouldn't leave him to collect an inheritance.

Or would she?

~

By the time Kathryn came back into the kitchen, Pete had had three hours to fret and worry about what she planned to do.

Her face was pale, her eyes swollen and red. He wanted nothing more than to wrap his arms around her and never let her go. That wouldn't take away her pain and sorrow, though. She had to deal with that herself. Time was the only thing that would help her.

He could ask her to stay, but he wouldn't. She had to make that decision for herself. If she wanted to leave, no matter how much it would hurt him, he'd let her go.

She sank down into a chair at the table and picked up the letter, reading it again.

"Would you like some tea now?" he asked.

She looked up at him and nodded. "Yes, thank you."

Pete was anxious to ask her about her plans, but he forced himself to keep quiet. Instead, he took his time preparing her tea and a minute or two later, he set a cup of hot, sweet tea in front of her.

"You need to eat something, too." He put a plate of shortbread cookies beside her. She picked one up, took a small bite, shook her head and put it back down on her saucer. "I can't."

"Okay, why don't I just leave them here in case you want one later?"

She nodded absently. Her fingers shook as she picked up the cup and sipped at the tea.

"Do you want to talk about it?"

She shook her head. "There's nothing to talk about," she croaked. "He's gone."

He was reluctant to ask the question that could change his life, but it was better to know right off than to wait, letting it hang over his head. "Are you going to go back to Ohio?" he asked.

She raised her eyes to meet his. "Pardon?"

"Ohio," he repeated. "Are you going back? It was in the letter."

"Oh… I forgot about that."

"Well?" He couldn't keep the worry that she'd tell him she was leaving out of his voice. "Are you going to go?"

Her grief-filled eyes gazed up at him for what seemed a long time before she answered. Then the words he'd been afraid to hear spilled from her lips. "Yes."

He could barely speak past the tightness in his throat. "When?"

"As soon as possible."

"I see."

He turned away, busying himself by putting the cookie tin back on the shelf.

It was over! She was leaving!

And if she was still holding onto her anger from their argument, she likely wasn't coming back!

125

CHAPTER 10

athryn choked back tears as the Austin train station—and Pete—disappeared from view behind her. She slumped back in the seat and closed her eyes.

He didn't want her. He didn't love her. She'd hoped and prayed that at some point in the four days between her telling him she was going back East and saying goodbye to him a few minutes ago, he'd ask her to stay. Tell her he loved her. Tell her to hurry back. At least tell her to come back.

But he hadn't said a word. He'd gone on as if nothing had changed. Done his chores the way he always did. Kissed her goodnight the way he always did.

He'd been particularly quiet on the ride to Austin from Sapphire Springs, but she hadn't felt much like talking either.

It had been even worse when they were standing on the platform waiting for the train to come in. Her heart was shattered that he seemed anxious to be on his way home, and when it had come time for her to board, he'd kissed her gently, wished her well, and let her go.

The train picked up speed. Strange, she thought as the landscape passed in a blur. She'd been so afraid of the future when she'd made the trip to Texas, and now, she was doubly afraid of the loneliness that awaited her in Ohio.

Kathryn shivered, tugging the crocheted shawl tighter around her shoulders.

She'd grown so used to the blistering heat of Texas summers that autumn in Ohio, which had always been her favorite season, felt like the dead of winter.

It wasn't just her reaction to weather that had changed. She knew that. The noise, the smell of coal in the air, so many people …

She missed Sapphire Springs. Missed the new friends she had there. Most of all, she missed Pete.

She loved spending time with Charlotte and the babies, though. She'd been shocked when she'd seen her again when she got off the train. Her once-vibrant sister was pale, stick-thin, and seemed to have lost all the sparkle she'd always had. It was understandable, she supposed. Not only had she lost her father, she'd lost her husband and father of her children.

"Here we are." Charlotte tucked her hand into the crook of Kathryn's elbow and led her across the street to the brick five-story building where their father's attorney was waiting to read the will.

A short time later, a stern-faced woman ushered them into the attorney's office, a room filled with dark cherrywood furniture, leather chairs and heavy drapes at the long windows. A floor-to-ceiling bookshelf along one wall held rows and rows of thick books.

The attorney, a short, heavy man with a face that reminded Kathryn of a cherub, stood up as they entered.

"It's nice to see you again, Charlotte." Turning to Kathryn, he introduced himself. "I'm Wilson Aberfoyle, your father's attorney. My condolences. Your father was a long-standing client of mine, and a friend."

"Thank you," Kathryn murmured.

The lawyer sat back down and shuffled a few papers from a pile on the desk beside him. Finally, he drew out a folder and opened it flat in front of him. "Mrs. Fallon, I assume your sister has explained to you the terms of your father's will."

"She has."

"Then let's get down to it." The attorney picked

up a pair of thick spectacles and put them on. "Your father had always hoped you'd come back to Ohio, but since you didn't, he wanted it to be clear that he expected you to upon his death. I did try to dissuade him, but he was determined.

"Your father's home is to be sold and the proceeds, along with all other income and investments, are to be shared between you and Charlotte. However, you must use part of your share to purchase a home here in Dayton and maintain the residence for at least five years."

"And if I don't?" Kathryn asked.

"Your share of the inheritance will be forfeited and turned over to your father's brother, Harry."

Uncle Harry! Kathryn hadn't seen or heard from the man in years, not since Uncle Harry had swindled more than a thousand dollars from her grandparents. The man was a ne'er-do-well, a scoundrel, and a criminal. Her father would roll over in his grave at the thought of his brother inheriting his estate.

The attorney leaned forward, steepling his hands on his desk. "I realize this might be a difficult decision for you. If you decide to stay and claim your share of the inheritance, in order to fulfill the terms of the will, I'll expect you to provide me with a copy of the agreement to purchase a home here before the funds can be released."

Charlotte leaned forward, resting her hands on the desk. "And the rest of the inheritance is Kathryn's to do with as she pleases?"

"That's right." Mr. Aberfoyle took off his spectacles and put them down, blinked a few times and turned to meet Kathryn's gaze. "Of course, if you do spend the money and then sell the house before the required time, you'll owe Mr. Higgins the entire amount you originally received."

Kathryn huffed out a sigh. She couldn't let Uncle Harry have the money, but staying in Dayton…

She missed Pete more than she'd thought it was possible to miss anyone. Her heart ached, especially at night. She'd grown used to having Pete's warm body beside her, hearing his soft breathing and occasional snoring. She missed his laughter, his teasing, his messiness. Even if he didn't love her.

"Do you understand?" Mr. Aberfoyle's voice interrupted her thoughts.

Kathryn understood only too clearly.

"Time is of the essence," he went on. "You have thirty days from today to provide the information. If you fail to do so, the funds will be released to Mr. Harold Higgins."

A month? What was she going to do?

Tinny notes from a piano in the corner of the saloon mixed with the voices and the occasional bout of laughter from five men playing poker near the stairs leading to rooms upstairs. Cigar smoke hung heavy in the air.

Pete sat alone at one of the scarred tables, the glass of beer in front of him untouched. He couldn't really say why he was sitting in a saloon other than that the house was too empty, too silent since Kathryn left.

She'd left a few of her belongings—a hairbrush, a half-empty bottle of rosewater, the two summer dresses she'd made while she was living in Texas. She'd taken everything else with her. When he was thinking rationally, he knew she'd taken the clothes she'd need while she was in Ohio, especially since she'd told him she didn't know when she'd be coming back.

She hadn't said she wasn't coming back. She hadn't even said "if" she came back. So why did his brain—and his heart—tell him he'd never see her again?

She'd been gone for almost a month, but he could still smell her, still expected to hear the sound of her voice singing off-key when he came into the house in the evening, still turned over in bed, expecting her to be lying beside him.

Even Lucky seemed to know something terrible had happened. While the puppies were growing and exploring the farm and the nearby fields, Lucky stayed close to home, as if she sensed Pete needed her.

After supper, when he went to the barn to take care of his chores, she followed, and when he sat on the porch in the darkness, she lay at his feet, looking up at him with those sad eyes—eyes that he was sure accused him of sending Kathryn away.

He lifted the beer to his lips and took a long swallow. As he set the glass back on the table, he heard John's voice. "Wondered if I'd find you in here again. You're spending a lot of time in here these days."

Pete shrugged. "What of it?"

John slid into a chair beside him, and gestured to the bartender, pointing at Pete's glass. "Not like you, that's all. Haven't heard from her, huh?"

Pete shook his head.

"What are you going to do about it?"

Pete met his concerned gaze. "Nothing. She didn't want to stay."

"Did you ask her to?"

"Why would I? She was pretty clear in what she wanted to do. Didn't hesitate for a second when I asked if she was going back. I wasn't about to beg. So I'm going to get myself drunk enough that I'll have to crawl home, and maybe even take one of the ladies upstairs to make up for what I've been missing all these months." He picked up his glass and took a long swallow of beer, catching the slight shake of John's head as he set the glass back into the water ring he'd left on the table. His gaze bothered Pete. "What?"

"Never thought I'd have a fool for a friend," he muttered.

Pete's temper surged. If John wasn't such a good friend, he'd have already bounded to his feet and planted his fist in his face. Instead, he gritted his teeth, wrapped his hands around his glass and concentrated on the foamy bubbles in his beer.

"Miranda told me what you said to Kathryn on your wedding night," John went on. "What kind of thing is that to tell the woman who's traveled hundreds of miles to marry you? Don't you think she was hoping you'd both fall in love eventually? Most women want that, you know."

"It didn't seem to upset her," Pete countered.

"Like she's going to tell you—a stranger—that she wants you to love her. I swear sometimes you don't have the brains you were born with."

"I just told her the truth."

"And is it?" John prodded. "Seems to me you wouldn't be sitting here getting pie-eyed drunk if you didn't care that she left. Seems to me that maybe you were wrong when you told her you'd never love her. Seems to me—"

"All right! I do love her." The words came out louder than he intended. Three men at a nearby table looked up from their card game to give him a knowing look and a smile, as if they'd found themselves in the same situation at one time or another.

Pete's face flamed. Lowering his voice, he continued. "So what if I do? It doesn't matter. She doesn't love me, otherwise she wouldn't have picked money over me."

"Wrong again," Pete said and took another sip of beer. "She does love you. She told Miranda that. You know I'm not a gambling man, but I'd bet she didn't leave because of her inheritance, but because she didn't want to spend her life with a man who didn't love her back."

Pete couldn't believe he was hearing right. "What? She did…does…?"

"That's what she told Miranda," Pete said with a nod. "I wouldn't be telling you this if I didn't think you could fix it."

Could he fix it? The only thing he could think of to do was to get on a train and follow Kathryn to Ohio and ask her to come home with him. She might refuse, but if John was right …

Hope gave him a lightness he hadn't felt in a long, long time.

Kathryn hurried down the street toward Charlotte's house. She'd been to the market a few blocks away and she was hot and thirsty, anxious for a glass of water.

A man climbed into a carriage in front of the house. As she approached, he gave her a half-smile. "Good day," he said. Then he flicked the reins and drove off.

She didn't recognize the driver, but that wasn't unusual. She didn't know most of Charlotte's friends and acquaintances.

"I'm back," she called out as she opened the front door. She set the basket containing the groceries on the floor and unpinned her hat, sliding the hat pin into the brim and putting it on the half-moon table in the foyer. Then she picked up the basket and made her way to the kitchen at the back of the house.

Charlotte was pacing the length of the room, her hands folded across her chest, her head bowed.

"Charlotte?" Kathryn frowned. "What's wrong?"

Charlotte looked up, her expression startled. "Oh…I didn't hear you come in…"

"I called out, but you obviously were lost in thought," Kathryn told her. "What is it? Has something else happened?"

Kathryn took in a shuddery breath, as if it took all her concentration. "I had a visitor just before you came in," she said.

"I think I saw him leaving. Dark hair, handlebar mustache?"

Charlotte nodded. "That does sound like him."

"Who is he?" Kathryn asked.

Charlotte dropped into a chair. "Owen's employer."

"What did he want?" Kathryn asked.

Looking up, Charlotte blinked, her eyes filled with unshed tears. "He came to tell me the bank expected payment for a loan they'd made to Owen." Her voice wavered. "Oh, Kathryn, I didn't even know he'd taken out a loan."

Wariness and mistrust niggled at Kathryn. It wouldn't be the first time someone had taken advantage of a recently widowed woman who was ignorant of her husband's finances. "Are you sure he really did take out a loan?"

"I'm sure," Charlotte said resignation in her voice. "He showed me the paper with Owen's signature. I'll be able to keep the house, but it'll take more than half my inheritance to pay back the loan."

Kathryn gasped. "Why did he take out a loan?"

"I don't know, but I have my suspicions," Charlotte replied.

"Oh?"

Charlotte looked away for some time, her gaze seeming to follow a squirrel scurrying along a tree branch outside. Finally, she turned back. Her voice softened. "Owen was a good man, but he had his vices," she began. "I'd rather not go into detail, but I will tell you those vices became more and more expensive over the years. I suspect the loan was to cover any debts he owed."

Kathryn was stunned. Owen had always seemed like a proper gentleman, responsible and straight-laced. It was hard to believe he would frequent bawdy houses, drinking establishments or gambling houses. "I'm so sorry, Charlotte, but don't worry. We'll figure something out."

Charlotte managed a weak smile. "It'll be all right. If I absolutely have to, Owen's family will take us in."

Knowing her sister and her children wouldn't be homeless made Kathryn feel a little better, but not much. Owen's family didn't think Charlotte was good enough for Owen, and they'd never bothered to hide their dislike. That she'd even consider relying on their charity told Kathryn just how dire the situation was.

Charlotte dropped into a chair at the table. "Have you decided yet what you're going to do?" she asked.

Kathryn shrugged. "No. I'll have to make a decision soon, though."

"When does Pete expect you back?"

"I'm not sure he does," she said miserably. "I miss him so much, but there's really no reason to go back. He doesn't love me, Charlotte, and I'm sure he doesn't care if I ever come back."

"What makes you say that?" Charlotte asked.

"He could have asked me to stay." A tinge of anger crept into Kathryn's voice. "He could have even forbidden me to leave. But he didn't."

The worry lines disappeared from Charlotte's face and was replaced by a determined expression. "I no longer have a husband, and even though I didn't love him—not really—I would give anything to have him back. You have a husband … you love him, don't you?"

Kathryn nodded. "Well…yes…"

"Does he know?"

"No," Kathryn replied. "I just couldn't…"

"So you left him without telling him how you feel or even if you were coming back to him?"

Kathryn nodded.

"Love is worth fighting for. I should have waited until I found a man I loved, but I didn't. I was wrong.

If you really love him, don't let your marriage die before it even has a chance—"

"It doesn't have a chance," Kathryn protested. "He told me he'd never love me."

"That was months ago," Charlotte pointed out. "Did you love him then? Did you expect to love him?"

"Well…"

"People change. Feelings change. The only way you'll know now is to ask him. Depending on his answer, you can make a proper decision."

Kathryn was still mulling over Charlotte's reprimand —yes, it had been a reprimand—as she opened the door to her father's house and stepped inside later that day. The silence was overwhelming.

She didn't belong here. Her life—her love—was in Texas. Could she be content to spend the rest of her life loving Pete, knowing he didn't love her back?

There had to be a solution. There just had to be. She still hadn't found one when she turned down the lamp and climbed into bed that night after a light supper. A faint breeze outside and a sliver of moonlight cast dancing shapes on the walls that reminded her of the trees that dotted the farm in Sapphire Springs.

She ached to see Pete again, but how could she leave her sister now? Should she go back to Texas and confess her feelings to Pete? Should she stay in Ohio?

She dozed off, sleeping fitfully until the first rays of dawn peeked through the curtains. Somehow, during the night, an idea had begun to form in her mind. As she lay awake, watching the shadows fade and the room fill with a golden glow, the details came together and she bounded out of bed, eager to put her plan into action.

CHAPTER 11

"Raised three boys in this house," Mr. Liscombe said as he and Kathryn strolled through the flower-laden garden surrounding a two-story frame house later that day. The house was much smaller than her father's house, only four bedrooms, a sitting room and a kitchen, but it was big enough. "Now that my wife is gone, there's nothing for me here."

"It's a beautiful house."

"Married forty-three years, we were," he went on, his voice growing soft and wistful as if the memories were taking over his mind. "We had our troubles and it wasn't always easy, but it was worth every minute of it. I just hope the folks who buy this house are as blessed as I've been."

Kathryn had decided the minute she'd walked through the front door that this was the perfect house.

"I'd like to buy the house, Mr. Liscombe," she said. "It's perfect."

Mr. Liscombe's wrinkles deepened as he smiled. "I was hoping you'd say that. I'll get the papers drawn up just as quick as a wink and the house will be yours."

Pete poked his head through the opening between the kitchen and the dining room of The Blue Sapphire. "Got any chicken and dumplings left?" he asked.

John looked up from the carrots he was chopping on the counter. "Not much, but you're welcome to have what's left in the bottom of the pot. What are you doing here anyway? I thought you'd be gone by now."

"I had to finish up an order for a hotel in Austin so I'll drop it off and catch the train on Friday," Pete told him.

"Makes sense," John agreed, wiping his hands on a cloth and picked up the ladle to spoon the chicken and dumplings into a bowl. "Got somebody taking care of the animals at your place?"

Pete nodded. "The dogs are at Stonehaven and Tucker Gates, the foreman, said he'd make sure the other animals were fed and watered."

"When will you be back?"

Pete shrugged. "I'll be back when I can convince Kathryn to come back with me."

"You want to eat here or in the dining room," John asked.

Pete slid into a chair at the kitchen table. "Right here's fine," he said, sitting back while John put his meal and two thick slices of bread in front of him.

"What if you can't convince her to come back?"

Pete didn't hesitate to answer. He'd thought about that every day since the day Kathryn left. He had only one choice. "If I can't do that, I'll be back as soon as I can to sell out and move to Ohio."

"That's a big step," John pointed out.

"That might be so, but if that's what it takes, that's what I'm going to do. She's my wife, and I'm going to do whatever I have to do to make her happy, even if that means I never see Sapphire Springs again."

Kathryn's heartbeat raced as Sapphire Springs came into view and the stagecoach finally rolled to a stop in front of the depot. Had she made a mistake? Should she have stayed in Ohio? She'd fretted about her decision the whole way, and now that the time had come, her legs trembled and her nerves grew as the driver took her hand to help her down.

The late afternoon sun painted the skin in pink and orange as she took in a few deep breaths to slow her heart rate and began walking through town toward the farm. With every step, she practiced what she'd say to Pete, taking into account every possible response he might have to what she had to tell him. Surely by the time she reached the farm, she'd be calmer.

"Kathryn?"

Her heartbeat skittered in her chest as she spun around.

Pete stood a few feet away. Oh, how she'd missed him! Suddenly, his arms were around her, holding her as if he'd never let her go, the stubble on his jaw grazing her cheek. "You came back."

She dropped her valise to the boardwalk and wrapped her arms around his waist. This was where she was meant to be!

After a few seconds, realizing they were drawing a crowd, she pulled out of his grasp. "Pete, people are staring."

"Let them stare," he said defiantly. "Let them see how glad I am that you're home."

Kathryn chuckled, a lightness filling her at his words. "I have something to tell you that I realized I should have told you before I left and that needed to be said in person rather than in a letter. That's why I came back, to tell you, but I'd rather do without an audience."

He nodded and released her. A frown creased his brow. Then he took her hand and tucked it into his elbow. "Okay. Let's go home."

❧

The wagon wheels squeaked. Birds chirped their goodbye to the day in the trees. The sun dipped beneath the horizon, painting the sky in fuchsia and orange.

Kathryn sat quietly on the seat while Pete chattered on about the latest happenings in Sapphire Springs while she was gone. Abner Eagleson's wife had had a baby. The Roberts boys had been caught stealing candy in the mercantile. They'd had a storm that tore the roof off Toby Laing's barn so the men had gotten together to repair it the weekend before.

She heard his voice but wasn't really listening, her mind too wrapped up in what she had to say once they reached the farm.

Finally, he drew the wagon to a stop in front of the house. "I'll just settle the animals and take care of the chores and then we can talk."

She nodded as she climbed down and lifted her valise out of the wagon bed. "I'll make coffee."

"That'd be real nice," Pete said with a wide smile. "I miss having coffee with you."

At least she had that, Kathryn thought as she went inside. Nothing had changed, other than there was a fine layer of dust on the furniture and Pete had left a screwdriver and a chisel on the table near the fireplace. A pair of socks were rolled into a ball and left under the sofa, and a catalog was opened and left face down on one of the chairs.

A soft smile tugged at her lips as she left her valise at the bottom of the stairs and made her way into the kitchen. She lit the stove, and after piling the dirty dishes on the counter, she pumped water into the coffeepot and added the coffee grounds, then put it on to brew.

The coffee was ready by the time Pete came into the house. He sniffed appreciatively and poured them both a cup. He put the cups on the table and closed the gap between them. "Why didn't you write or send a telegram to tell me you were coming home? I thought you'd left me, that you weren't coming back."

"I…wasn't sure I was going to," she said quietly.

His eyes darkened and a muscle in his jaw tensed, but he didn't respond. Instead, he took her hand and led her to the table. "Sit down and tell me what happened."

Kathryn told him everything, the visit with her father's attorney, the will, Charlotte's discovery that her husband had been in so much debt. Pete listened carefully without interrupting until she outlined the plan she'd devised.

"You gave away your inheritance?" he asked, his eyes wide.

She nodded. "Sort of," she said. "I fulfilled the requirements of the will, so I do own a house. The terms of the will stated I had to maintain a residence in Ohio. It said nothing about living in that residence. Papa's attorney was taken aback at my suggestion to let Charlotte and the children live in the house but since there was no requirement that I lived in the house, there was nothing he could do about it. That way, Charlotte could then sell her house and the proceeds, along with what's left of the inheritance after Owen's debts are paid, would be enough to support them for some time."

Pete leaned back in his chair and whooshed out a breath. "And you gave her your share as well."

"Most of it," she admitted. "I did keep some for us if we need it in the future, and I do own I house that I can sell after five years if I want to. I suppose I should have consulted you first, but Charlotte did promise to return the money I gave her if you objected."

"I don't object at all," he said. "I told you when we first got married that money isn't important to me. I'll admit I'm a little surprised, though. Most people would never do what you did."

"As I told you when we first married as well, money isn't important to me either. And she needs it more than I do."

"So you're staying here?" he asked. "With me?"

"We'll see," she replied. "My sister pointed out that there was something you needed to know—and I needed to know—before I made a decision."

"What is it you need to tell me and that you need to know?"

Her throat tightened. This was it. This was either going to be the most wonderful moment of her life or the most devastating. She had to draw on every ounce of courage she possessed to find out. "She told me I needed to tell you how I felt about you, about our marriage, about everything, before I decided what to do."

"Before you say anything else," he began, then got up and dug a piece of blue paper out of his pocket, "I have something to tell you. I know I told you the day we got married that I'd never love you, but I was wrong."

"What?" Could she really be hearing him right?

"I do love you," he repeated. "I don't know how it happened. It sure wasn't supposed to happen, but it did. I didn't realize it…or maybe I just didn't want to admit it, but I do. That's why I was going to get on the train on Friday to go to Ohio and bring you home."

"You love me?"

He nodded, and for a moment or two, she thought she saw moisture in his eyes. "More than anything."

"You were coming to Ohio?"

He handed her the train ticket. "I figured I'd rather live in Ohio with you than in Sapphire Springs without you."

She looked at the ticket, blinking through her tears then smiled up at him.

"What did you want to tell me?" he asked, worry in the tone of his voice.

"I…I love you, too," she said softly, then repeated it. "I needed to tell you that I love you. I think I started falling in love with you the first time I saw you. And every day, I grew to love you more. When I was in Ohio, I couldn't imagine spending the rest of my life without you. Charlotte made me realize that I needed to tell you in person, so that if you didn't feel the same way, I could go back to Ohio and live with her and the children."

He got up and came around the table, drawing her to her feet. He kissed her soundly, crushing her against his chest. Her breath caught in her throat, her emotions making it impossible to breathe, only to feel his lips on hers, knowing his kiss was one of love, not the kiss of a dutiful husband.

Her insides tingled. Her knees threatened to buckle. When he finally released her mouth, her breath came in ragged gasps.

"From now on, the only time you're going back to Ohio is for a visit, and I'll be going with you," he said.

"I like that idea," she said, her smile so wide it hurt. "Are you sure you don't mind about the money?"

"I have something worth more than all the money in the world," he told her. "I have you."

Tears of happiness trickled down her cheeks. "There is one other thing…"

His smile faded. "What?"

"You once told me that I'd have to tell you straight out when I was ready to consummate our marriage," she began.

He grinned. "I said that, didn't I?"

"You did say that." She stood on her tiptoes and gently brushed her lips over his. "Pete Fallon, I love you. I want to have your children and grow old with you. But right now, I really really want to be a real wife to you."

In one swift movement, he scooped her off her feet. She let out a squeak of surprise and her arms snaked around his neck as he headed toward their bedroom.

As he gently placed her on their bed, she looked up at him, seeing the love in his dark eyes. She smiled, her heart filled to overflowing. This was the way a marriage was supposed to begin—with love and hope for the future.

From now on, this would be the day she'd always think of as their true wedding day.

EPILOGUE

"I have a surprise for you," Pete said, his eyes twinkling with mischief and a wide grin on his lips as they rode back to the farm from Sapphire Springs a few weeks later.

"You do?" Kathryn shifted in her seat, searching the wagon bed for a package or some sign that he might have bought a gift for her. She'd been in town all day helping Miranda to sew new curtains for the diner windows while Pete made a delivery in Austin. "What is it?"

"If I tell you, it won't be a surprise, will it?"

Kathryn couldn't imagine what it might be. There was nothing she needed, and even though they had a nest egg now, there wasn't anything she wanted badly enough to spend it.

Her excitement grew, and as soon as Pete drew the wagon to a halt in front of the house, she climbed down and raced up the stairs.

She threw open the door and hurried inside, then stopped dead. Her eyes widened and she let out a gasp. "Ohhh…" Her fingers touched her lips. There, on the wall where a bookcase used to be, was a piano.

In shock, she crossed the room and gingerly pressed one of the keys. The sound filled the room. Overcome with happiness, she turned to face Pete, who'd come in behind her and stood a few feet away. "How…why…?"

"Do you like it?"

She grinned. "I love it. But—"

"Good," Pete said. "I hope you don't mind that I spent some of your money—"

"Our money," she pointed out.

"I know you miss playing, and when I saw it in a shop in Austin, I couldn't resist buying it."

Kathryn threw herself into his arms and kissed him soundly. "Thank you, but you might be sorry you bought it," she said when he released her.

Pete's smile disappeared. "Why?"

"I might be too busy playing to cook and clean and look after the baby," she said.

"I doubt…what? What baby?"

"You're not the only one with a surprise."

Pete's face paled. "You're…?"

She nodded.

"I'm going to be a father?" he asked, his voice little more than a whisper. Then much louder and with a grin that seemed to fill his face, he shouted, "I'm going to be a father!"

He cupped her chin and kissed her. "We need to have John and Miranda for supper and share the news. If it hadn't been for Miranda…well, really, if it hadn't been for John inviting me to supper, trying to match me up with Agatha Trimble, I never would have even thought about getting married and now I'm going to have a son or a daughter, too."

Kathryn's heart almost exploded with emotion. Her thoughts shifted to her father. Tears stung her eyes, but they were tears of happiness, not grief. Because of him, she had everything she'd ever dreamed of—a husband who loved her, a home of her own, and soon, a child.

"Thank you, Papa," she whispered, then wrapped her arms around Pete's waist and snuggled close.

Lifting her face to his, he kissed her tenderly, and she knew this was where she was meant to be.

Forever.

ABOUT THE AUTHOR

Margery Scott is the author of more than thirty sweet western historical novels, novellas and short stories. An avid reader, she didn't even consider writing her own books until her three boys were grown and she had an empty nest.

She now lives on a lake in Canada with her husband, and when she's not writing or traveling in search of the perfect setting for her next novel, you can usually find her wielding a pair of knitting needles or a pool cue.

Website: www.margeryscott.com
Email: margery@margeryscott.com
Newsletter: www.margeryscott.com/newsletter
VIP Facebook reader group: www.
facebook.com/groups/margeryscott